SWORD AND BOW

A Quest to Save Alfham

SWORD
AND
BOW

JEFF DENONCOUR

WORLDCHANGERS
M E D I A

I am dedicating this book to my family for believing, first of all, that my stories should be written, and secondly, for encouraging me to write them.

Table of Contents

A Quest to Save Alfham ...

CHAPTER ONE
Picking Out the Tree

Christmas was approaching and the boys were getting very excited. It showed in everything they did. The littlest job that their parents asked them to do around the house was done without the usual prodding. Their schoolwork was completed and put away before Mom called them down for dinner.

Even with the busy schedule for Mom and Dad, the week before Christmas was a joy. Now, this isn't to say the other fifty-one weeks of the year were not enjoyable—they were just different.

The Gillis family, plus their dog Muffin, lived in a small town known as Manchester-by-the-Sea. It's a sleepy little village on the coast of Cape Ann, bordering what used to be the fishing capital of the world, Gloucester, Massachusetts, and a twenty-five-minute drive to the bustling city of Boston. But no matter how many times the family made their way into the city, which was not very often, they loved their life in their sleepy little town.

Jeff was twelve and Sam was nine, the perfect ages for taking in all the wonders of the Christmas holiday. Today, Dad had promised to take them to a special place to cut down their own Christmas tree. It was the same tree farm Dad had gone to when he was a little boy. It was in the town of Boxford, about a half hour away from their house. Dad told them how he used to cut down his own tree at this tree farm every year. In the boys' minds, this place had become magical, and their excitement could hardly be contained.

"Boys, we had better get going before all the great trees are taken," Dad said to Mom with a wink.

"We put the saw and the rope in the truck," Jeff said.

"Great, let's get going," Dad told them.

As they headed out the door, Mom gave each of the boys a little snack for the ride. "We'll see you later," they said to Mom.

What a day! Christmas carols were sung, the sun was shining, and there wasn't a cloud in the sky, but as they got closer to the tree lot, the clouds started to move in.

"What is it with these clouds? It was supposed to be a beautiful day," Dad said. Soon after, they noticed the first spitting of snow flurries and, before they knew it, they were driving through a white blanket of snow.

"If this place wasn't just up the road, we'd have to turn around," Dad said.

Jeff pointed to a sign on the right. "Dad, that sign says Parker's Tree Farm." As they drove in, disappointment registered on the boys' faces when they saw a man putting out the closed sign.

"Do you think he'll still let us cut our tree?" Sam asked.

"I don't know," Dad said. "Let's ask him."

They drove the truck up to the man and asked if he could stay open for a few minutes while they quickly cut their tree.

"Sorry, even if I stayed open a while longer, the cutting lot is about a ten-minute walk from here and you would still need to pull your tree out with a sled," the man advised them. "The way this storm is coming in, you'd have a difficult time dragging out your tree."

"I understand," Dad said. "Do you think you'll be open tomorrow?"

"I hope to be. Christmas is next week and there are a lot of people who still haven't got their trees cut."

It was obvious that the man was right. The storm was getting worse, and the snow was starting to pile up. Dad knew he couldn't take the chance with the boys, even if their hearts were set on getting the tree today.

"Well, boys, I think it best if we head home before this storm gets bad."

The boys took it better than he thought they would. "Do you think we can come back?" Jeff asked.

"As long as it's not snowing, we'll definitely come back tomorrow," Dad said.

Disappointed but hopeful that tomorrow the sun would shine, they drove off into the storm. As the wind whipped the snow into a frenzy, it started to make the driving treacherous. Dad turned on the radio to see if he could get a weather update and found a station that was delivering the weather. According to the announcer, a surprise snowstorm was hitting the area. No one saw it coming. They said the storm would start about mid-morning and intensify into a full-blown blizzard.

"Guys, it looks like we'll have to buy a tree from the place near our house," Dad said.

"That's alright, Dad," Sam said.

Jeff chimed in. "We don't mind. After all, it's still a Christmas tree."

Hearing these words from his boys lightened Dad's heart and made him very proud.

As they drove along, the boys stared out the window at the snow-covered landscape. "I think the snow's stopping," Jeff said.

As Sam turned to look out Jeff's window, it suddenly stopped. Not another flake fell. It was as if someone had placed a large roof over the entire area. And just as the snow stopped, the boys spied a sign: "Azar's Christmas Tree and Toy Store next right."

"Hey Dad, can we stop there?" Sam asked.

"You know, I've been down this road at least a hundred times and I don't ever remember seeing this sign," Dad said with surprise. "I wonder if it's a new store. Well, it can't hurt to see what's down there." He put on his blinkers and turned down the dirt road.

Soon they came to a small building. The outside of the store was old and dilapidated. The windows were so dirty that you couldn't see inside. The place could have done with a paint job, the roof needed to be repaired, the porch was missing floorboards, and as far as they could see, there were no Christmas trees. But for some reason, they all still felt hopeful, like everything was going to work out perfectly. Dad parked the truck, and Jeff and Sam jumped out.

"Hold on and wait for me," Dad said as the boys rushed onto the front porch.

As they entered the store, a blast of heat hit them, and the scent of hot chocolate and woodsmoke filled the air.

It reminded Dad of walking into his home when he was a little boy. There was always a fire burning in the wood stove and the smell of home-cooked meals in the air.

As he took the first few steps into the store, Dad did a double take. As dilapidated as the outside looked, the inside was incredible. The floors and walls were built out of old, wide pine boards. There was a narrow timber staircase leading to a balcony floor that wound its way around the building. Behind the staircase, a long, wooden counter filled with all sorts of odd contraptions lined the wall. In the middle of the store stood a large wood stove. Next to the stove was a neatly piled stack of wood and two rocking chairs atop a braided rug. A wooden box sat between the two chairs. The whole scene looked very welcoming.

While Dad was admiring the stove, the boys were mesmerized by all the toys. They'd never seen the types of toys that covered every shelf in the store. These toys were different: there were no electronic gadgets, plastic movie characters, or video games to be seen. Instead, there were pull carts, horse-drawn wagons, and wooden swords and shields. There were bows and arrows hung carefully on a rack. Almost every item was carved from wood.

"Sam, look at the back wall," Jeff said, his eyes widening.

When Sam looked over, his jaw nearly hit the floor. There, all along the back shelves, were carvings of ogres, fairies, goblins, and unicorns painted and sculpted so realistically that they almost seemed alive. But what captivated Sam and Jeff the most were the figurines of the dragons. They seemed so real that the boys approached them with caution, feeling that, at any time, they might get blasted by a plume of hot fire. But as they got closer and tentatively touched the toys, their nervousness disappeared, and a feeling of happiness came over them. They soon forgot about the disappointments of the day.

"Can I help you?" said a strong, gentle voice from behind the counter, startling Dad, who turned to face a man with a gray beard and long, gray hair. The man stood up and walked out from the counter, a large, shaggy dog following behind

him. The dog's fur was as black as night, in quite a contrast to his master. The dog lumbered over to the boys and seemed to take an instant liking to them as they petted him.

"Hi, my name is Azar," the gray-haired man said. "Nice to meet you." The two men shook hands. "There aren't too many people that Herschel takes a liking to so quickly. They must be special boys."

"I certainly think so," Dad said. "Your sign out front says that you're selling Christmas trees, but I didn't see any."

"Oh no, I don't leave my trees out front," Azar told him. "I keep them in the back. You see, they are a special kind of tree. I don't sell them to everyone. As a matter of fact, I don't sell them to anyone. I give them away, but only to special people. Would you like to see one?"

The boys were quietly listening to the conversation, but when they heard this invitation they quickly let their opinions be known. "Dad, can we please see them to get one for home?" they asked in unison.

"Well, if it's okay with Azar, it's okay with me," Dad said.

Azar nodded his approval and said, "Follow me."

They walked toward the end of the building to a back door. Azar grabbed his coat, and they left the building. He pointed to a path leading into the woods. "It's only a short distance."

The snow had covered everything in a blanket of white. The trees were heavy with the weight of the snow and the branches formed a tunnel over the path. As they walked down the trail, all they could hear were the sounds of the woods. Two squirrels quarreled over the few remaining acorns they could scavenge. A blue jay squawked out his territory. The wind blew through the branches of the pines and, occasionally, you could hear a big thump from newly fallen snow. It was very peaceful.

Then suddenly, all the sounds stopped—the wind, the birds, the squirrels, everything. There was silence in the forest.

Azar stood still. He took off his hat, turned his head toward the wind, and listened. The wind came as a distant whisper through the trees, seeking an ear to tell its story to. As it passed over the travelers, it lingered for the briefest of moments, and then it was off again. Soon, the sounds of the forest returned, and everything was back to normal.

"That was odd," Dad said.

They'd just resumed their walk down the path when Azar turned to ask the boys if they'd heard anything. They looked at each other, and Jeff said, "We heard the wind, but it was very strange. It seemed like someone, or something, was calling for help."

"Hmmm, very peculiar, "Azar said, bobbing his head up and down. "Yes, very peculiar indeed."

Soon they came to a small cabin located in the middle of the forest, and next to the cabin stood a lone tree.

"There it is," Azar said proudly.

"Is that the only tree you have?" Dad asked.

"Didn't you only need one tree?" Azar said.

Dad walked slowly around the tree. "I must say, this is the most perfectly shaped tree I've ever seen. And I can't ever remember seeing one with such a spectacular color of green."

Azar smiled. "As you can tell, there will never be a tree that will be its equal."

CHAPTER TWO
The Presents

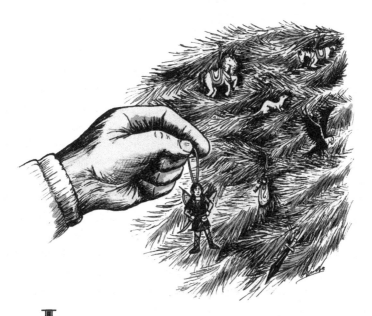

I t was a beautiful tree. The branches were perfectly shaped. The color was stunning. Even though it was a beautiful shade of deep green, the tree radiated a bluish glow, and the needles were velvety soft to the touch. But more than anything, it was the healthiest-looking tree they had ever seen.

"Dad, this tree would be perfect," Jeff said. "It's not too tall or too wide. You know how Mom is always worried about the size of the tree."

"Do you think we'll have enough room to fit all of our ornaments on it?" Sam asked.

"Oh, yeah! We may even have room to spare," Jeff said. "It has a great top. We won't even need to trim it to put on the Christmas Angel. Wait a minute, this tree is alive!"

"Azar, we can't take this," Dad said. "It would be terrible to cut down this tree."

"You are so right," Azar agreed. "It would be terrible to cut even one branch. That's why this tree has never seen the blade of a tree pruner. I told you that my trees are special. As you can see, I've planted it in an old wooden barrel so that it can be moved. If you take this tree, you must promise me that you will never cut it down. In the spring, you must find a safe place to plant it. If you do these things, you'll give it a chance to be a strong and vibrant tree. It will be a home to birds and many other creatures, but mostly, it will help keep our air clean and pure."

Azar pointed to the top of the tree. "Do you see the lone pinecone at the top? In this tree's life, it will produce thousands of cones, providing food for animals and producing many more trees. However, the first cone that it produces is very special. Its seeds will be the strongest and most productive that it will ever bear. The cone protects these seeds and will not open until the time for planting is near. When the cone opens, you must take the seeds and plant them. They will grow fast because they come from a very special tree."

"Where should we plant them?" Sam asked.

"When the time comes, you will know when and where," Azar said. "If you can accept those terms, I will allow you to take the tree."

Before Dad could reply, the boys cried in unison, "We accept!"

"It's a lot of responsibility, you know," Dad said.

"We can do it, Dad," Jeff said. "We feed Muffin and take her out for a walk every day."

"And we do our chores most of the time," Sam added.

"Okay, you're right, you are pretty good at doing your chores," Dad said. "That settles it. If we have your permission, Azar, we would like to take the tree."

Azar turned and looked directly into both boys' eyes. In that instant, he understood things about the boys that most people would not know in a lifetime. "Yes, I think that you two would be fine caretakers for my tree. It is done. You may take it."

"How do we get it down to the truck?" Dad asked.

Azar took a whistle out of his pocket and blew into it. No one heard a sound from the whistle, but soon Herschel came bounding out of the woods. "You see that sled over there?" Azar said. "We'll put the tree on the sled and let Herschel pull it out for us."

Together, they lifted the tree onto the sled and began their walk back to the store. As they left the woods, Sam asked if they could go into the store and look at the toys one last time.

"Let's get the tree into the truck first, and if it's not snowing, we'll take a quick run back into the store," Dad said.

After putting the tree in the truck, they all went back into the store, welcoming the heat as it had gotten colder during their walk in the woods. They each hung up their coats, and then Azar put a few more logs on the fire.

"I have a nice pot of hot chocolate sitting on the stove and it should be about right for drinking," Azar said. He poured everyone a cup and then sat down in the rocking chair, inviting Dad to sit next to him.

"I've been wanting to do this ever since I came in the door," Dad said with a smile.

Azar nodded. "It's a very cozy set-up. Boys, come over and sit with us. Besides the tree, there's something else that I would like to give you." He pointed to an old wooden box beside the stove. "The toys in this box are very special to me and I only give them to very special people." He bent down and took the cover off.

When the boys saw what was inside the box, their eyes opened wide as they gazed at the most amazing toys they had ever seen. There were miniature replicas of horses, swords, forest animals, and many other amazing creatures.

"Where did you get these?" Jeff asked.

"Oh, I have had these for a long, long time. I can't remember where I got them, but I have had them for as long as I can remember. You know, more than once, I've used these items to decorate my house. I believe they would make great ornaments for your Christmas tree. Would you like to take a few of them home with you?"

Jeff and Sam were so excited that they could barely control themselves.

"How many can we take?" Sam asked.

"You can take as many as you want," Azar said.

So as not to break any of the items, the boys were very careful as they explored the contents of the box. Sam's first choice was a small leather pouch that contained a pure white vial and a large red key, which he chose because it had a replica of a dragon at one end. Sam was always drawing dragons, even at school when he should have been paying attention to the teacher.

Jeff, on the other hand, chose a wooden sword that had a blade blacker than pure coal and a handle wrapped in leather straps. It reminded him of the sword in one of his fantasy games.

Then they each chose a horse. Sam chose the pure white horse, while Jeff picked the black one.

As Sam picked up his horse, he looked it over carefully and then sniffed it. "Azar, this smells just like a real horse."

"Mine does too," Jeff said.

"Isn't that peculiar. Well, we know they're not real," Azar said to Dad with a smile and a wink.

Lastly, each of the boys chose an animal. Jeff picked out an eagle because he enjoyed learning about birds. He loved walking in the woods trying to determine what kind of bird he was hearing by its call.

Sam picked out a ferret because it reminded him of his warrior foxes.

"These are great," Jeff told Azar. "Thank you very much."

"Yes, thanks a lot," Sam said.

"Would you like to take a few more items?" Azar asked.

"No, thank you, I'm all set," Jeff said.

Sam looked over the toys and shook his head. "Me too. Thank you very much."

"Jeff and Sam, I believe that you have made some very nice choices. You know, the decisions that you make in life have all kinds of consequences, just like the gifts you have chosen today. Each of these toys is special in its own way, and only you know why you chose them. There may be a day when these gifts play a larger part in your life than you could ever expect, and I believe that you will know what to do with them when that time comes."

Dad gave Azar a bewildered look, trying to understand what he could mean.

"There is one last gift that I would like to give the

two of you to share," Azar told the boys as he rummaged through the box.

At the very bottom, he found the item he was looking for. When he pulled it out of the box, the boys became very excited.

"Sam, did you see that in the box before?" Jeff asked.

"If I had seen that, I would have remembered," Sam said.

It was the most realistic-looking elf they had ever seen. It had all the dressings and gear that one would expect an elf to have: a beautifully curved sword hanging from his belt, a bow with arrows strung across his back, a dagger, and a pouch attached to his waist. His cloak was dark brown, and the rest of his dress was that of a woodsman. He was so lifelike that they half-expected him to stand up and walk away.

As the boys took their presents from Azar, they noticed that the box seemed to refill itself. When they looked back again, Azar had closed it.

"Well, we'd better get going. How much do I owe you for the tree?" Dad asked.

Azar smiled. "Oh, goodness, I don't charge anything for my trees. If you take care of it, that's all I need for payment."

"Well, thanks again for everything. You sure did come to our rescue," Dad said.

"Maybe we'll see you next year for another tree," Jeff said.

"No, this is my last tree, and I won't be back again. But maybe someday, I will see you again."

After saying their goodbyes, Dad and the boys walked back to the truck and made sure that the tree was secured for their journey home. As soon as they got in, the snow began to fall again. As they started down the road, the boys turned to wave goodbye to Azar, but through the falling snowflakes the view of him slowly faded and soon they were looking at a haze of white.

It was also getting dark. Dad glanced at the car clock and realized how late it had become. "I'd better call Mom and let her know we're on our way home. She's probably wondering what took us so long."

If he had looked in the back seat, he would have seen that the boys were so totally engrossed in the gifts Azar had given them that they hadn't heard a single word he'd said.

Due to the storm, it took them a while to make it back home. By the time they pulled into their driveway, it was dinnertime and the snow had stopped.

"Do you think we'll have enough time tonight to decorate the tree?" Sam asked.

"Let's get it in the house first, and then we'll see what Mom has planned," Dad said.

Getting the tree into the house was no small chore. With the boys' help, Dad was able to pull it out of the truck and maneuver it into a wheelbarrow. He slowly wheeled it up to the front porch and together they lifted it up to the front door. As the tree was much taller than the doorway, it got stuck halfway through. Dad wasn't worried about the needles going all over the floor since it was a live tree, but he was still very careful because he didn't want to break any of the branches.

Mom came out of the kitchen to help. "Hon, I'm going to pull the barrel out and you bend the top branches down," Dad said. "That should get it in."

At first, it didn't move. "Pull it down a little more," Dad said.

Once Mom pulled the branches down so the top could slide in, the tree was finally in.

They all heard something fall, but when they scanned the floor, they couldn't find anything. What they hadn't seen was the pinecone being ripped off the top of the tree as it passed through the doorway and falling under the small table at the bottom of the stairs.

"Well, that's quite the tree," Mom said. "But what's it doing in a wooden barrel?"

"That's a long story. I'll explain later," Dad said.

Before Mom could say another word, the boys bombarded her with a detailed account of the day's events.

They told her about the snow, the hidden store, the walk through the woods, the tree, and Azar, the nice man who owned the store. Lastly, they showed her the gifts he had given them.

"It sounds like you had quite the adventure today. I'll bet you're so tired that you want to go straight to bed," Mom said with a little twinkle in her eye.

"No, we're not tired," Sam said, while Jeff just gave her that "what are you talking about, it's only nine o'clock" look.

"Well, if you're sure," Mom joked. "While you were gone, I was able to get all the decorations down from the attic. Let's eat dinner and, if it's not too late, we'll decorate the tree."

Later, as they sat in front of the decorated tree and admired their handiwork, the boys realized they hadn't put the presents Azar had given them on the tree.

"Dad, can you hang our ornaments near the top?" Sam asked. "I want everyone to see them."

Dad hung the ferret, the eagle, the pouch with the vial and key, the sword, and the two horse ornaments right near the top, and then placed the elf carefully in the middle.

"What do you think?" Dad asked.

The boys both gave him the thumbs-up sign.

"I think this is the prettiest tree we've ever had," Mom said. "It smells so nice that it's almost like being outside."

They sat and gazed at the tree for a few more minutes until Sam started to yawn.

"Well, fellas, I think you've had quite the day," Dad said. "I'd say it was time for bed."

"I'm not tired," Jeff said. "I just want to go upstairs and play my video game for a while."

"Okay, but just for half an hour and then to bed," Mom said.

Sam yawned even more—he loved his bed and never protested about going to sleep.

The boys left their warm seats in front of the tree and started upstairs. Just as they got to the top, Sam realized he'd forgotten his favorite Beanie Baby on the coffee table and ran down to get it.

Sam and his best friend, Dan, had created an army of Beanie Babies. Their favorites were the warrior foxes— they were the fighters. With help from Dad, they would cut pieces of copper and create all sorts of accessories like swords, shields, helmets, and armor to outfit their soldiers. Then they would let their imaginations take them and their fighters on different adventures.

Near the front door, Sam noticed that there was something under the table next to the stairs. When he bent down and felt under the table, his fingers touched something hard and sharp, but not very heavy. He picked it up and realized that it was a pinecone. *Now where did that come from?* he wondered. Suddenly, he understood. He turned and looked right at the tree. Where the pinecone should have been, hung the elf that Azar had given them. The cone had fallen off the tree.

"Oh no!" Sam exclaimed.

"Sam, what are you doing?" Mom called. Without thinking, Sam put the pinecone into the large front pocket of his sweatshirt and hurried upstairs. He took off his sweatshirt, put on his pajamas, and jumped into bed.

As he lay there, he started to think about the day's adventure and, before long, he had fallen into a deep sleep, dreaming of fighting dragons and other creatures alongside his warrior foxes.

Jeff, on the other hand, went past the half-hour curfew, lost in the fantasy world of his favorite video game.

CHAPTER THREE
Finding the Adventure

The week before Christmas passed painfully slowly for the boys, but finally, the school events, family gatherings, and all the little extras had been completed. Christmas Eve was here.

As tradition had it, they always spent that evening at their grandparents' house with all their cousins, uncles, and aunts. Usually, the festivities started in the early afternoon and ended in the late afternoon, but tonight, they went late into the evening. When someone looked at the clock and realized how late it had become, they all decided that it was time to leave, for Christmas morning would soon be here. With the celebration over, they all journeyed back to their homes.

On the drive, Jeff and Sam scoured the sky for any possible sighting of Santa's sleigh. With every light that appeared in the distant sky, Sam insisted that it was Santa and that they needed to hurry home.

When they got home, Mom and Dad prodded the boys upstairs to get ready for bed. With Christmas morning just hours away, the boys were wide awake and ready to stay up. But, as you can imagine, Mom was having no part in that.

"Now remember, the quicker you get into bed and get to sleep, the faster Christmas morning will come," Mom said, giving a sly smile and a quick wink to Jeff. The boys ran up the stairs and were ready for bed in no time. They came back down to kiss Mom and Dad goodnight, and then they hurried back up and jumped into bed.

Even though they had their own bedrooms, Jeff and Sam always slept in the same room together on Christmas Eve. They would build a tent made of an assortment of blankets to sleep under. Sam had a bunk bed in his room, and this made making the tent much easier. They tied blankets around the bedpost with their bathrobe belts and then tucked the other end of the blankets into a bureau drawer, forming a perfect tent. Next, they took the cushions off the window seat, covered them with multiple blankets and other assorted pillows, and *ta-da*, a perfect bed. For them, nothing was as soft and cozy as this make-shift bed, but for an adult, sleeping there would result in a visit to the doctor.

Lastly, they placed a small flashlight between them so they could see each other while they talked late into the night, imagining what Santa might bring them.

This year, whether it was the desire to fall asleep quickly or whether it was magic at play, they were both sound asleep soon after their heads hit the pillow.

On their way to bed, Mom and Dad checked in on the boys. "Christmas Eve and they're asleep before ten o'clock," Mom said with surprise.

After pulling down the tent, Dad gently shook each of the boys awake and helped them get into their real beds. Sam always slept on the top bunk and, in his groggy state, Dad had to help him with the ladder. Jeff stood up and sort of fell into the bottom bunk. Both of them went back to sleep immediately. On the way out, Dad left their door open just a crack.

"In case they wake up, it will make it easier for them to sneak downstairs," he said to Mom with a little grin.

Soon all the lights had been turned off and the only sound was the soft breathing of the slumbering family.

Suddenly, Sam sat up. *Did something move in his room*

or was he dreaming? He could have sworn he'd heard something. Sam was a very light sleeper and the slightest noise woke him up at night. He sat perfectly still and looked around the room, listening for the slightest out-of-place sound. Nothing. All he could hear was the wind trying to squeeze itself through the windows and enter the warmth of the house. He had a final look around and put his head back onto the pillow, but as soon as he shut his eyes, there it was again. He sat bolt upright. Rubbing his eyes, he looked down at Jeff to see if he was awake and moving around, but Jeff was sound asleep. The only stirring was the slow up-and-down movement of his breathing. "I must be dreaming," Sam said to himself.

With his heart pounding in his chest, he gave the room a final once-over. Seeing only shadows cast from the moonlight shining through the window, he closed his eyes and went back to sleep.

Shortly after, Jeff woke up. He looked around the room wondering why it was still dark. It should be close to morning; however, the clock on the nightstand proved otherwise. It was only 10:50 p.m. *I guess it's still early to be getting up*, he thought, so he turned over and tried to go back to sleep. He tossed and turned in his bed, the events of the week still fresh in his mind. He couldn't stop thinking about all the exciting things that had happened. Finally, at about 11:30, Jeff decided to see if Sam was awake.

"Hey, Sam, are you up?" There was no reply from the upper bunk.

He waited a few minutes and tried again. This time, he called a little louder, and just for good measure, he kicked the underside of Sam's bed. That was something only an older brother would do.

"Hey, Sam, are you awake?"

"Is it time to get up?" Sam asked groggily.

"No, but I can't sleep. I keep thinking about what happened at Azar's store last week."

Instantly, Sam was awake. "I have to say, that was a cool day. I think my favorite part was seeing all the toys in Azar's special box."

The boys talked for a while longer and, before they knew it, they both started to yawn.

"What time is it?" Sam asked.

As Jeff turned to tell Sam it was midnight, they both heard a small bang outside their room.

"Did you hear that?" Sam asked.

Jeff sat up. "Yeah, it came from downstairs."

"Maybe it's Santa. Do you think we should go down and check?"

"No, what if it's Santa? If he sees us, he might not leave any presents," Jeff said.

Sam nodded. "You're right, let's wait a little longer. If we don't hear anything, we'll go down and check it out."

The boys waited for a few more minutes, and when they didn't hear any more noises, they decided to investigate. When they got out of their warm beds, the cold air hit them hard. They both looked for something to put on. They found the sweatshirts they had worn to the Christmas tree shop rolled into the corner and threw them on.

Sam slowly opened the door, and they poked their heads into the hallway.

"Do you hear anything?" Sam whispered.

"No, I think the coast is clear."

The stairs leading down to the first floor were right outside Sam's room. At the bottom of the stairs and to the left was the large living room where they kept their Christmas tree.

As the boys stood on the landing, they noticed a bluish glow radiating out of the living room and streaming up the stairs.

"What do you think that blue light is?" Jeff asked.

"Maybe Mom left the lights on the tree so that Santa could see," Sam whispered back.

Jeff crept toward the stairs. "No, that can't be," he said. "We have colored lights, not blue ones. It's something else, but I don't know what. Maybe we'd better check."

Before the boys went down, they stopped and listened one last time. Not hearing anything, they continued their

investigation, Sam secretly hoping he was going to catch a glimpse of Santa. They could never have guessed what they were about to discover.

About halfway down the stairs, they peered through the railing into the living room and saw their dog Muffin sitting on her haunches, tail wagging, staring at the tree. But what they also saw next was very strange.

An aura of bluish light emanated from the tree. It wasn't coming from a single source, like a candle or a light bulb, but rather, the whole tree was glowing blue.

"What do you think it is?" Jeff asked.

Sam looked at him and shrugged. "Look at all of the presents," he said excitedly.

With all the presents under the tree, the lure was too much. Muffin came to greet them as they walked into the living room but kept turning to look at the tree.

Suddenly, Sam grabbed Jeff's shoulder. "I just saw something move in the tree."

"Where?"

Sam pointed. "Right by that large present. Maybe it's a mouse."

Jeff grabbed a pillow from the couch in case there was a mouse. Slowly, the boys pulled away all the smaller gifts sitting in front of the large one. But as they were about to grab the big present, Sam pulled Jeff back and they both fell to the floor.

"What are you doing?!" Jeff exclaimed, a little bit irritated.

"Something is climbing up the tree," Sam said, and they advanced again.

"Where?"

"Do you see the baby's first Christmas ornament? It's right in there." Sam pointed to a spot halfway up the tree, but whatever it was, it had stopped moving.

In order to see inside the tree, Jeff began to fold away the branches carefully, so as not to break any of the ornaments. When he got a clear view of the trunk, he saw something *very* peculiar. There, sitting on a branch, was a little man kicking his feet back and forth as though he had been waiting impatiently to be discovered.

The boys immediately recognized the elf that Azar had given them at the store. Normally, upon seeing a two-inch elf sitting on a branch of a Christmas tree, the average child would run screaming to his room, lock the door, jump into bed, and wait for whatever nightmare he was having to come to a complete stop. However, we aren't talking about your average kids. Jeff and Sam had imaginations larger than life. During their playtime, they created incredible adventures. They would often journey to the far reaches of enchanted worlds where they would battle dragons, fight orcs, and encounter many other strange and exotic creatures. So, seeing this little elf was more of a dream come true than a frightening incident.

Now, it may have been a totally different experience if they hadn't been influenced by the prior week's events, specifically Azar's store.

The elf said something, but the boys only looked at each other.

"Did you hear what he said?" Jeff asked.

"No, I couldn't hear a word."

Jeff looked back at the elf and cupped his hand to his ear. The elf motioned for them to come closer. The boys practically had their heads inside the tree, only inches away from the elf.

"Can you hear me now?" the elf yelled.

"Barely, but we can hear you," Sam said.

"Who are you?" Jeff asked.

"Who I am doesn't matter, but what I have to ask of you is extremely important!" exclaimed the elf. "Meet me at the bottom of the tree and I'll explain what we must do. Quickly now!"

The elf scampered down the tree. When he got to the bottom branch, he jumped onto the bucket that held the tree, tied a rope to a branch, and shimmied down the rope to the floor.

The boys moved the big present out of the way so they both had enough room to see the elf. They lay down on the floor so they could be eye to eye with him—sort of.

"Come closer," the elf yelled, and the boys inched forward. They were so close now that their noses were almost touching him.

Suddenly, Muffin squeezed in between Sam and Jeff, knowing that something was going on. When she saw the little man, she let out a yip.

"Muffin, stop," Jeff whispered as he pulled her away from the tree and made her lie down next to Sam and the elf.

"Now, let me tell you who I am and why I am here," the elf declared.

CHAPTER FOUR
The Answer

"My name is Mas, son of Yenneb," the elf said. "I've been sent here by King Olim to bring you back to our world. Something terrible is happening in our land and we need your help."

The boys looked bewildered, so Mas continued. "I will explain, but I must be quick, for we must be on our way. My world used to be beautiful and green. The forest went on forever, as did the grasslands that surrounded it. The water in the rivers was as clear as the skies that overlooked them. It was a wonderful place to live. All our people lived together and shared in the land's wealth. Then, some of our people started to abuse it. Greed contaminated them. Our people took and took, but we never returned anything back to our world. Soon, sicknesses infected everything. Our world became dark. Years of war destroyed what beauty was left, and then the land started to die. Some people, those of a pure heart, could see what we had done and started to change things. But so much damage had been inflicted on our world that even they gave up. That is, except for one: King Olim's daughter, Princess Iris. She is not only beautiful, but her heart is beautiful. She brought back light and hope, which began to spread among the people, and soon our world started to heal. The fields around her home started to turn green again. There was hope that the world could change, and with it, the people's spirits lifted.

"Then, the black day came. The forces that had taken control of our kingdom, like the Boitus, didn't want this change, so they found a way to poison the Princess. They infected her with a terrible illness. Soon after that, our hopes faded, an evil returned to our world, and the decline continued."

Mas gazed at the boys sadly. "Princess Iris still lives, but she is in a deep sleep. I am afraid she will soon perish and, with that, so will our world."

"If all is lost, why do you seek our help?" Jeff asked.

"The King's wizard believes that he has found a cure for the Princess's illness. There is a tree that produces a very special cone, and he believes that something in the seeds will cure her."

"So why don't they just go and get them?" Sam asked.

"Remember what I said earlier: everything in our world is dying. Up until now, we thought that all those trees had perished. But then, stories started to filter into our kingdom that some of these trees still existed in the northernmost regions of our world. The King sent his armies with the bravest knights to retrieve the cones, but alas, only a squire returned to tell the story. He told King Olim that he had seen a beautiful forest full of the trees that would cure Princess Iris, but he also told another tale: the story of a great dragon, black as night, with pure evil coursing through her veins."

"If all of your best knights have failed, how will you retrieve what you need?" Jeff asked.

"We can't," Mas said, gazing up at them. "We are hoping you will."

Jeff looked back at Mas with surprise. "Us? But we are only boys. We don't know anything about fighting dragons!"

"When the Princess first fell ill, she had a vision, or so we thought. She kept saying this phrase repeatedly: *"JEF-SAM-Brothers will help."*

"In our language, *JEFSAM* translates into 'bringer of life.' Finally, the King's wizard went to the old books and found a reference to this word, a tale of two brothers, true of heart, young of age, and wise beyond their years. Together, they saved a perishing world. Their names were Jefrus and Samion."

"As you know, or maybe not, all our worlds are connected. There is energy that flows freely from world to world. With skilled magic, the great wizard searched all the worlds to find brothers named Jefrus and Samion. When his search failed, he realized that the names could be translated differently in other lands. So, he kept searching, and that is when he found three sets of brothers, all from different worlds. They all possessed traits similar to Jefrus and Samion. The King sent three groups of his most trustworthy subjects, each containing a wizard and a warrior, to seek out these boys and see if they would help save our world. I am the last warrior. The other two have failed. In their search, they found that all of the brothers were old men and did not have the strength to overcome the passage into our world. You two are our last and only hope." Mas looked deeply into each boy's eyes. "Will you help us?"

"How can we help?" Jeff asked.

"You must travel with me to my world. That is the only way," Mas replied.

'Travel to your world, how?" Jeff asked.

"I will take care of that. I only need to know if you will help us," Mas said.

Sam and Jeff both stood up.

"What should we do?" Sam asked.

Jeff shook his head at this brother. "Sam, he is asking us to go to a different world—that's crazy. Christmas is tomorrow. What will Mom and Dad think when they wake up tomorrow morning and find us gone?"

"I know," Sam said. "We can write them a letter telling them that we will be back shortly and not to worry. After all, Mom and Dad always tell us that we should help those in need."

"I'm sure they didn't mean to go into a different world. We don't even know how long it will take us or how long we'll be away."

Suddenly, a lightning flash went through the room. The boys looked down at Mas and saw him motioning them to come lower. They both lay back down as the elf spoke.

"Don't worry about that," he said. "Time in our world goes much faster than in yours. We will be back before dawn comes here. If it takes us longer than that, all hope for our world will be lost."

Usually, Jeff made decisions very slowly and deliberately, as if he were crossing the "t's" and dotting the "i's" before making up his mind. As a child, it would take days of prodding from Mom just to convince him to change from winter long-sleeved shirts to summer short-sleeved shirts. But once a decision was made, there was no turning back.

Sam didn't make rash decisions, but, on the other hand, they weren't as well thought out as Jeff's more careful decisions. To him, if the consequences didn't get him into trouble, it was at least worth trying.

"Are you sure we'll be back by morning?" Jeff asked.

"I can't be sure of anything," Mas said. "There are dangers ahead, but I will do everything I can to protect you and see that you return to your home by morning."

Jeff thought for another moment. "Sam, are you sure you want to go?"

"I am," Sam said.

So, ignoring the fact that Christmas would soon be here and that they could soon be opening their presents, Sam and Jeff said in unison, "We'll go!"

Mas heaved a sigh of relief, for he had not known what to expect from these two boys.

"Where is your land and how do we get there?" Jeff asked.

"The name of my land is Alfham. As to how we get there, leave that to me."

The elf reached into a pouch that was tied to his waist. He grabbed something that looked like silver dust and blew it at Jeff and Sam. The sparkling powder hit them directly in the face. Surprised, they closed their eyes and tried to move back, but they were frozen in place as they started to experience a very strange sensation.

When the boys were finally able to open their eyes, everything around them was getting larger. The tree and the presents surrounding them were becoming enormous. The room itself was becoming cavernous. Then suddenly, it all stopped. There they stood, under the tree, not knowing what had happened. Had they shrunk or had everything else grown?

The elf popped up from behind one of the smaller presents and said, "Oh, there you are! It was much easier to find you when you were bigger."

"What happened to us?" Sam asked.

Before Mas had a chance to answer, they all heard booming footsteps coming toward them. They looked up to see Muffin sniffing around the tree.

"Quick, run to the back of the tree before she steps on us!" Jeff yelled.

Thank goodness Muffin hadn't stepped on them, or worse, gobbled them up like she did with crumbs that fell on the kitchen floor at dinnertime.

"I blew shrinking dust on you," Mas said, panning his hands to show them everything in the room. "Need I say more? You know, I once blew so much dust on another elf that he disappeared. I had to spread a whole pouch of enlarging dust on the floor to find him."

"But why did you shrink us?" Jeff asked.

"Well, if you stayed as big as you were, you would never fit inside the door," Mas said.

"What door?" Sam asked.

Mas pointed straight up. "It's at the top of the tree, and we'd better get going. It's getting late."

"Oh, okay, then let's go!" Jeff said.

The boys looked up. From where they were standing, their Christmas tree reminded them of the trees they had seen on their trip to Muir Woods in California, where some of the tallest trees in the world exist. It seemed that reaching the top of their tree would be impossible.

"How do you expect us to get to the top?" Sam asked Mas.

"First, we must climb up the rope to reach the bucket that holds the tree."

Mas had very powerful arms and was able to scamper up the rope as quickly as he had slid down it. For the boys, it was a little more difficult. Sam tried it a couple of times but kept slipping. Finally, Jeff told Sam to watch him.

"We did this in gym class," Jeff said.

He showed Sam how to place his feet on the wall of the bucket and slowly walk up the wall. Soon enough, Sam had mastered the technique, and Mas was able to grab his hand and pull him to the top. Jeff followed fast on his heels, and soon they were all together.

Now, the boys looked up and realized that the climb had only begun because the top of the tree still seemed infinitely far away.

"We have to climb up on those branches," Sam said, "but they seem awfully far apart."

"We obviously have to climb the tree," Mas said, "but this time, we'll have a little help." He grabbed another pouch that was tied to his belt.

What Mas pulled out was not a powder, but a thick paste that smelled like a pungent evergreen candle, the kind that your parents would light at Christmas. Mas moved to the base of the tree and liberally spread the paste across the bottom. He then traced his fingers over the trunk in a spiraling motion for as far as he could reach. Within seconds, the tree started to tremble, and suddenly thick limbs sprouted from the sides, each about the length of a baseball bat. They spiraled up the tree at an amazing speed, creating a perfect staircase for as far as they could see.

The staircase was sturdy, and the three quickly ascended the tree. They were close to the top when Mas told them to take a break. He grabbed a burlap sack out of his backpack, and with the nimbleness of a tightrope walker, he ran down the entire length of a branch. He threw some of his shrinking dust on a few items that were hanging from the branches, grabbed them, and threw them in the sack.

Quick as a wink, he made it back to where the boys were sitting and said, "Alright, let's get to the top."

They climbed until they could go no further. At this height, the branches were becoming thinner, and they could see the whole living room from where they stood. They could see Muffin staring up at them, tail wagging, tongue hanging out, and every once in a while, they could hear a little whimper.

As tightly as they could, the boys held onto the trunk of the tree. They had never climbed this high before, and the tiny tingle that was running up and down the backs of their legs confirmed how scared they were.

They could see that Mas was looking for something at the very top of the tree. The branches were wedged in close together, creating a circular platform that allowed him to walk around the upper part of the tree. He kept going around and around, feeling the outer bark.

"I know it's around here somewhere," Mas kept muttering.

"What are you looking for?" Sam asked.

"I am looking for a keyhole. You can only see it if you have specially trained eyes. So, just stand there and I will find it."

"What does the keyhole look like?" Jeff asked.

"It is very similar to a knot that you would find on any ordinary tree," Mas replied, a little annoyed by the boy's inquiries.

Jeff pointed to an area next to a small branch about five feet above them. "Is that it?"

Mas saw where he pointed and said, "Ah, there you are. I knew I would find you."

Sam and Jeff looked at each other and smiled. They were becoming very fond of Mas.

Mas jumped up to the branches above him, reached into a little pocket on his cloak, and pulled out a small key. As he placed it in the keyhole, a very bright glow outlined the shape of an intricately carved door. When he opened the door, a beam of light was released from the entryway that was so bright that the boys had to avert their eyes. Almost instantly, the light faded. Where there was once a beautiful door now stood a gaping black hole.

Mas looked at them and said, "Come now. We must leave."

The boys climbed to where Mas stood. They clung to the trunk of the tree, staring into the black hole.

Mas tried to comfort them. "There is nothing to fear and I will be with you at all times. We are about to embark on a very perilous journey, but do not fear this darkness, for this is not where the threat resides. You must trust that I will always tell you the truth, no matter what the consequence. But more importantly, trust what your heart is telling you."

The boys could tell by the way Mas had spoken that what he said was the truth.

"All you must do is jump inside. At first, it will feel strange, but no harm will come to you. When you land, you will be in Alfham. Remember, trust what your heart is telling you."

Then Mas jumped.

Jeff and Sam went to the edge of the entrance and looked down. There was nothing but blackness—but this time, it didn't seem so threatening. They could smell the sweet scent of spruce, which brought back memories of when their dad took them hiking in the White Mountains. This was one of their favorite things to do with him.

"Well, it can't be all that bad," Jeff said to Sam.

Suddenly, they heard the voice of Mas calling to them. "Well, are you coming or not? We don't have all day!"

The boys looked at each other and held hands. As they jumped, they heard the clock's chime strike midnight. Christmas was here.

CHAPTER FIVE
Into Alfham

They didn't have the feeling of falling, but rather, it was more like floating, like a down feather floating from the sky. The blackness turned to different shades of color. It was like falling through a rainbow. They could still smell the scent of spruce but now it was mixed with a different odor, and by the time they realized what it was, they had landed with a bump.

All they could smell was the decaying odor of rotten wood.

"Can you see anything?" Sam asked Jeff.

"Not much, but I think we're in some sort of tunnel. I see a faint light at the end."

"Where do you think Mas is?"

"I don't know, but let's get out of here," Jeff said.

The boys began to creep toward the light and soon found themselves crawling through a constricted passageway. As they reached the end, they peered out of the opening, and there, sitting next to a roaring fire, was Mas, a stout-looking horse, and a few sacks.

"Well, young masters, it's about time," he said. "I thought I was going to have to eat all by myself." A pot of grains, dried fruits, and herbs stewed over the fire. It smelled absolutely delicious.

The boys walked over and sat next to the elf. The night air was chilly, and they welcomed the warmth of the fire. Looking back, they could see that they had crawled out of a massive log, like a picture of the giant sequoia trees from an article in *National Geographic*. The trees were so large that you could drive a truck through their trunks.

"Where did the horse come from?" Sam asked as they dug into their meal.

Mas glanced toward his horse. "He is an old but loyal friend of mine. He has been waiting for me to arrive back from your world. Might I say, he was getting a little impatient for my return." The horse bobbed his head and snorted.

When they'd all finished eating, they worked together to set up a lean-to shelter, then went back to sit by the fire. The stunning view overlooked a very wide and deep valley. In the western sky, an almost full moon was rising above the tree line.

"Look at the size of that moon!" Jeff said. "It looks twice the size of our moon."

"If you think that's special, look to the east," Mas said, pointing eastward. There, another almost full moon was rising above the horizon.

"Two moons, that's crazy! Have you ever seen anything like that, Sam?" Jeff asked.

"No, and they're huge," Sam said.

"But even more amazing than that is what you're going to witness in a few days," Mas said. "A spectacle that occurs only once in ten lifetimes in our world. Both moons will be full, and they will pass through each other's path."

"Is it like an eclipse?" Jeff asked.

"I know what you mean by an eclipse, but it isn't like that. Each moon passes halfway through the other. The merger of the two moons makes it look like one gigantic orb, but the strangest thing is that it appears to be blue. The light that it emits allows you to see everything. It will be so clear that you will think it's daytime."

"That is so cool," Jeff said.

"How can the light be blue when the moons look white?" Sam asked.

"I've heard that it has something to do with the way the combined light hits our world's atmosphere, but I am not really sure," Mas answered.

As they sat there looking into the night, the light of the two moons allowed them to see for miles, but something about the view troubled Jeff. He stood up and peered out over the valley. Wherever he looked, the trees were bare. Not one single leaf hung from the tiniest branch. It reminded him of the pictures he'd seen of the devastation from the eruption of Mount St. Helens back in Washington. "Is it winter here?" he asked.

Mas shook his head sadly. "No, it is early spring in our world. The buds on the trees should be sprouting but our world is slowly dying. This is what the death of Alfham looks like."

"And I don't hear any crickets, owls, or any other night creatures," Sam said. "It's like there's no life out there."

Mas cocked his head and looked at the boys. *These two might just be the ones that save our world*, he thought to himself. He threw them each a sack. "Here, take these clothes. They'll make your travels much more comfortable."

Jeff opened his sack first and started pulling out items that were similar to what Mas was wearing: leggings, soft boots with padded soles, a natural white tunic that would reach to mid-thigh, a poncho-style outer garment, and a leather belt to keep everything in place.

The boys changed into their new clothes, which were surprisingly soft and comfortable. They both opted to keep their sweatshirts on rather than putting on the ponchos.

"You may want to keep that outer garment," Mas told them. "If the weather turns bad, they will keep you warm and dry. They're made from the fleece of the Igwart goats who withstand some of the most extreme temperatures in our world. They live in the Dungovin Mountains, where in the winter the cold can freeze a man's breath. Your pants and boots are made from the same fleece."

The boys nodded and put the ponchos over their sweatshirts. They were about to toss the sacks back to Mas when they realized they weren't yet empty. Sam reached in first and pulled out a sword, a bow with a quiver of arrows, a knife attached to a belt, and a leather pouch. He opened the pouch and took out a small white vial. He opened the vial and sniffed, but there was no odor, so he couldn't tell what was in it.

"Be careful with that," Mas cautioned. "It is said that the contents of that vial will help bring our world back from the darkness. I do not know how, but it is said that only the carrier will know when and where it should be used."

Sam realized the pouch resembled the one Azar had given him at the store. Suddenly, he felt the weight of the world on his shoulders. He closed the vial and placed it back in the pouch. He tried to hand the pouch back to Mas, but Mas refused to take it from him.

"But how am I going to know what to do with it?" Sam asked.

Mas patted Sam on the shoulder. "I am sorry, young one, but that responsibility has been passed to you and your brother by powers greater than me. This burden is yours and yours alone. Trust in yourself. When the time comes, you will know when to use it."

Sam lowered his head. *I hope so with all of my heart*, he thought.

CHAPTER SIX
True Gifts

After seeing what Sam had retrieved from his sack, Jeff became very interested in what could possibly be in his. He too found a bow with a quiver of arrows, a knife, and a pouch. But the sack was still heavy, so he reached in and touched something at the bottom that was cold and hard. As soon as he grabbed it, whatever it was became warm in his hands. As he pulled it out of the bag, he could see that it was a sword. The blade was as black as coal and so polished that he could see his reflection in it. The handle fit his hand perfectly. It had small ridges that passed along the length, and there was a circular hole at the very end that almost looked like a bite mark.

Jeff held up the sword, staring at it in wonder. "In all of the video games and adventure movies I've watched, I've never seen a black blade on a sword before."

"Nor will you ever again," Mas said. "There has only been one sword that was ever made like it. It was fashioned from the scales of a dragon's tail. Some say that the dragon still exists. The legend says that a young man was trying to save his village from the wrath of a black dragon, a particularly fierce and powerful beast that roamed this world many years ago. Most dragons killed to eat and survive, but this dragon killed for pleasure. All the people lived in fear, for they knew that one day the dragon would come and destroy their village, as he had done to so many others.

"A group of the bravest villagers decided to take action and hunt down the dragon and slay it. They traveled to the North country, where the dragon lived in a deep cave, high in the mountains.

"A month passed and when none of them returned, the families mourned their deaths. But one young boy whose father had been part of the group tried to convince the people of the village to go to the mountain and see if any of their family members were still alive. Even with all his pleading, no one would go with him.

"The boy knew that dragons had long memories and that he would not forgive the village that had sent men to kill him. So, one evening the boy went to his father's blacksmith workshop and found the special sword his father had been making for the King. Knights from all over came to him for their swords, for no one was his equal in forging them. When the boy held the sword, he felt the strength of his father course through his body and, at that moment, he knew what he must do. He would go and kill the dragon."

"He went all by himself?" Sam asked.

Mas nodded. "Yes, he was very brave, but maybe a little bit foolish."

"I'd say so," Jeff said.

"Now let me finish the story," Mas said. "The boy traveled for days and finally came to the dragon's cave. It was very dark but scattered about the cave were small pools of fire, which provided him enough light to see his way into the dragon's lair. The boy could only smell the dragon, but the dragon could see the boy very clearly, as they have perfect sight, even in the dark. From stories his father had told him, the boy knew that the only way to avoid a dragon's fiery breath was to move away as soon as he heard the dragon inhale."

"How did his father know so much about dragons?" Jeff asked.

"According to the tales, the father was a dragon hunter in his younger days and had killed at least three dragons. As the boy walked further into the cave, he could sense the dragon's closeness. Suddenly, the dragon took a deep breath and blew a length of orange fire right at him. The boy barely escaped the dragon's breath by jumping behind a rock. However, the blade of his father's sword was the one thing that did not escape the dragon's fire. It glowed as red as it had the day his father had forged it. If it had not been made of the purest metal, the sword would have instantly melted into a pool of liquid iron. Without thinking, the boy grabbed the handle of the sword, burning his hand."

"It really must have hurt," Sam said. "I touched a stove top once and burnt my hand."

"I can guarantee you that it hurt, but he didn't have time to think about that," Mas said. "He wrapped his leather pouch around the sword's handle, creating a perfect grip. This time, when he picked it up, it was only warm, a warmth that reminded him of his father's love. He felt stronger than he had ever felt before.

"The boy stood up and faced the dragon. He yelled, 'You killed my father, but you will kill no more.'

"Suddenly, the dragon swung its enormous tail at the boy, but the boy managed to jump away and hurl his sword at the dragon. The sword missed the dragon's body but became lodged under the scales of its tail. The heat of the sword was so painful that the dragon roared and bit off the end of its tail, leaving it lying on the ground. As the dragon reeled in pain, the boy grabbed the sword and ran deeper into the cave. The dragon soon followed with a rage only a dragon could feel.

"The dragon actually bit off its own tail?" Sam asked.

"Sam, be quiet and let Mas finish the story," Jeff said.

Mas continued. "When the boy reached the end of the cave, he hid behind a large rock. He could hear the dragon coming closer. As he looked down at his sword, he saw that something amazing had happened. The blade and the scales from the dragon's tail had fused together and become a glittering black blade. He grabbed the sword and accidentally hit the rock that he was standing behind. To his astonishment, the blade cut through the rock like a heated knife through butter. This, he realized, could pierce the thickest dragon scale.

"From the stories his father had told him of dragon lore, he remembered that a dragon can only die if its heart is pierced. Unfortunately, that is also where the dragon's scales are the thickest. Before a dragon can spill flame, it must first breathe in, and at that moment and only at that moment are they vulnerable. You see, as its chest expands with air, the scales that are over the heart become weaker as they become thinner. The boy knew it was then that he must strike—and strike hard."

"Do you remember the movie we saw about dragons?" Sam asked Jeff. "It's true that it's the only way to kill a dragon."

Mas and Jeff both looked at Sam with exasperation for all his interruptions, and Mas continued the story.

"The boy could hear the dragon's slow, rhythmic breathing and he knew the dragon was waiting for him to show himself. But because the cave was so vast, no matter how hard the boy listened, he couldn't pinpoint where the dragon was concealing himself.

"From where he hid, he could see the outlines of another large boulder, only feet from where he stood. He steeled his nerves and jumped from his hiding place to behind the other boulder. Just as he did, a cone of fire blasted his new fortress.

"Now that he knew the location of the dragon, the boy tossed his bag out in the dragon's direction so that he could get the dragon to breathe in before spilling his flame. He heard the dragon take a deep breath. This was when the dragon was the most vulnerable. The boy leapt from behind the rock and hurled his sword right at the dragon's heart as it inhaled.

"The dragon knew that it had been tricked and was ready to blast the boy with another cone of fire, but he was stopped short by the blazing sword piercing its heart. When the boy heard a terrible cry and a loud thump, he let out a deep sigh, for he knew that his sword had hit its mark. He came out of his hiding spot to see what he had done. There, lying in the middle of the cave, not moving, was the fearsome black dragon."

"The boy cautiously approached the dragon, as they are very cunning, and he knew the dragon could rise up and kill him. But that is not what happened. The creature did not move or take another breath. The boy had slain the dragon. But its death did not bring the joy he thought it would, but rather, it brought him a deep sadness. To his amazement, the dragon's body suddenly began to shimmer, and then it turned to dust."

"When dragons die, do all of their bodies disappear like that?" Sam asked.

"No, only the oldest dragons turn to dust," Mas said. "As soon as the boy went to retrieve the sword from the cave floor, everything started to shake, and rocks began falling from everywhere. He knew he had to get out of the cave that second, even if it meant leaving behind the sword. And there was something else that the boy left as he ran out of the cave—a small, oval egg, which was protected by a stone overhang. He barely made it out before the cave completely collapsed."

"The story of the black sword which killed the mighty dragon was passed from land to land, until my people finally heard the tale. They realized that the sword was special and that it should be protected, so they traveled far to reach the place where the sword was buried. After years of digging new tunnels in the mountain and searching for the sword, they finally found it and brought it back to our kingdom. Our people have kept it hidden and protected until the day when it would be needed again. Like the vial, the sword will play an important part in bringing our world out of the darkness."

"Was the egg a dragon's egg?" Sam asked.

"We believe that it was, and we did look for it," Mas said. "However, if we had found it, we would have destroyed it. Dragon's blood is passed through the mother. If the mother is evil, its offspring will receive all of its traits tenfold, and we couldn't imagine this creature roaming our world."

"Did you ever find it?" Jeff asked.

"No, it was never found," Mas said.

After hearing the story, the boys stared up into the night sky and seemed to be in a world of their own. Suddenly, they heard branches breaking in the forest. Mas joined them as they stood and fixed their eyes on the dark forest. Something was coming, and it was coming fast.

The light of the two huge moons cast strange shadows over the forest, so no matter how hard they tried, they couldn't see what was barreling toward them. What finally appeared out of the darkness shocked them all: two horses, one as black as coal and the other white as newly fallen snow, trotted out. The horses were not very large, but they were very muscular.

"Sam, these horses look like the ones at Aunt Sue's farm," Jeff said.

Sam nodded. "They also look like the horses that Azar gave us at the store."

Before they could say another word, they heard a loud screech coming out of the night sky. Sam pointed and yelled, "Look up there!"

Soaring high above them was a huge eagle. One could make out its enormous size against the bright moons. The wingspan must have been nine feet or more. Suddenly, it dived toward the camp. The boys scrambled and jumped behind an enormous log, but Mas stood calmly with one arm sticking out straight. The eagle slowed its descent and landed on Mas's arm.

The eagle was clutching a small animal in one of its claws. It was long, thin, and brown. The boys could tell that the little creature was alive, but it didn't seem to be trying to escape. Mas gently took the animal from the eagle and placed it on his shoulder. The eagle flew onto a nearby tree branch.

"I think it's a ferret and an eagle," Jeff said.

"You are correct, young master," Mas said. "The ferret is known as Cerith. She is the most cunning and the most loyal of all the ferrets to ever come out of the land of Yarlsling."

At that moment, Cerith jumped off Mas's shoulder and ran to Sam, looking up at him. Sam bent over and picked up Cerith, who immediately ran up Sam's arm and sat on his shoulder, nuzzling his ear.

Mas smiled. "It looks like Cerith has chosen you as her travel partner. She chooses those who are kind to all creatures. You should consider yourself fortunate, for she is very particular."

Mas then reached into a pouch that was tied to his belt and pulled out a small wooden object.

"What is that?" Jeff asked.

"It is a whistle," Mas said, but when he blew into it, no sound came out.

"What kind of whistle is that?" Jeff said. "It doesn't make any sound."

Suddenly the eagle flew from its perch on the branch and landed on Mas's arm. She sat there, twisting her head back and forth. "She comes to the call of the whistle that only she can hear. She is known as Windsong. Her speed is unsurpassed by any eagle in this land. Both Windsong and Cerith have been my dearest travel companions for many years. We have had many adventures together and, at one time or another, we have saved each other's lives."

Then the two horses walked over and stood next to Mas.

"What are their names?" Sam asked.

Mas patted each of the horses. "The black one is called

Storm and the white one is called Promise. They are both stallions from opposite parts of this world. They bring with them courage and stamina far beyond that of an ordinary horse, for in their world, they are kings."

Storm trotted over to Jeff, brushing against him, while Promise came to Sam and nuzzled her head against his. Jeff and Sam both stroked the horses' necks.

"It looks like they have chosen their riding partners," Mas said. "Come, let us sleep. We must rise early, for tomorrow we start our adventure, and I fear in the days ahead we will get very little sleep."

* * *

The boys woke to something warm and wet rubbing against their faces. They opened their eyes, half-expecting to see their mother giving them a kiss, but instead, they were quite surprised to see horses standing over them.

"The sun will be rising soon, and we must be on our way," Mas called to the boys.

Morning came quickly to the camp, but the warmth of Jeff's sleeping blankets tempted him to roll over and go back to sleep. "Mas, I've done a lot of camping, but this is the most comfortable sleeping blanket ever," Jeff said.

Sam nodded in agreement.

"It was made from the wool of the Balaria sheep," Mas

explained. "Their fleece is tough and knotty, but once it's combed and treated, it becomes soft and light as a feather. It provides warmth during the coldest of nights, protection from the rain, and a shield against the rays of the hottest sun."

The boys got up and stretched, then settled on a log with the hot tea and biscuit Mas handed them. Once they'd finished, they began to gather their belongings. They rolled up the few remaining items of clothing they would carry inside their sleeping rolls, and then fastened them to their saddles. The saddles were much smaller than what they'd used back home and had many loops and leather straps.

"Those are traveling saddles," Mas told them. "They are light and sturdy, and you can fasten your equipment to the rings."

When the boys put the saddles on their horses, they saw that they fit each horse's body perfectly.

"It looks like it was made for my horse," Sam said.

"No, it was not," Mas said, "but it could have been. These saddles are the best in the known world. The Eljab people make them. They live far to the West and treat their horses as part of their families. When a child reaches its sixth year, a yearling is given to them. From that day, they must feed and take care of it as if it were their own child. A bond develops between the two that is so close that when they ride, it looks as though they are one. They have developed these saddles so that there is little discomfort for the horse, no matter the length of travel."

After securing all their belongings to the saddles, the boys mounted the horses. Now that the sun was rising, they could see the land they had come to visit. They walked the horses over to the edge of the precipice. From this vantage point, they had a panoramic view of the landscape, and all they could see was death. But far to the north rose a snow-capped mountain range. From this distance, the mountain range seemed small and insignificant, but in their hearts, the boys knew that it would be the battleground for whether life continued or ended for the world of Alfham.

CHAPTER SEVEN
To the North

"Where are we going?" Sam asked.

"North, to the mountain," Mas said as he urged his horse forward.

The day had turned bitterly cold, and the sun was obscured by gray clouds. The land was flat, and traveling was easy. Other than the snow-capped mountains far in the distance, shades of brown dominated the landscape. Winter fields of long grass stretched out for as far as the eye could see, supplying the horses with all the food they needed. The fields presented enough rodents for the ferret and the eagle to claim an evening meal.

Mas and the boys journeyed in these conditions for days, until Jeff finally said, "We haven't seen any people. Does anyone live here?"

"This area of our world is known as the Plains of Drun. You can travel through these grasslands for days and never see its end. It is where many of the wanderers lived. They would set up temporary camps and bring their animals to feed for the summer months. A few villages border rivers to the South, but most people have left because the land no longer supports the wild horses and other animals."

"That's too bad," Jeff said. "I bet it was like the great grassland in our world. I read in a book that thousands of buffalo once roamed our prairies and then people killed all of them for their hides."

"That is also very sad," Mas said. "I guess those kinds of things happen in your world as well as ours."

"What other types of people live in your world?" Jeff asked.

"Mostly Elvish folk. I am a member of the High Elves, and so is King Olim, Princess Iris, and the people living in this region. We are a warrior society, but we do not like war. We fight only as a last resort. Some use magic to enhance their lives, but most of us don't."

"Do you use magic?" Sam asked.

"No, I don't," Mas said. "Then there are also the Wood Elves. They live a simple life, very in step with the natural world. Seeing nature destroyed was too much for them. They left this area many years ago in search of a better world. They haven't been seen or heard from for many years. I hope they found what they were looking for."

"I do, too," Sam said.

"When we enter the Canyons, a few days' ride from here, we may encounter Wild Elves," Mas said.

"What are they like?" Sam asked.

"They too remain close to nature," Mas said. "They live a very natural life, and they are rarely seen by others. They view outsiders with suspicion, but they are fierce allies of those whom they consider friends. They are the largest of all elves. They call themselves the Garish."

"Do they consider us as friends?" Sam asked.

"It's possible, for I had an encounter with them earlier in my life. But that story is for another day," Mas said.

The boys fought the boredom of the landscape by reciting the verbal drills that Mas had been teaching them about battle. They looked forward to the end of each day, knowing that no matter how tired they were, Mas would teach them more about the use of the sword and the bow.

He would always start out with the same message: "Just like your mind, a weapon can be very powerful. The greatest masters always think before they strike. However, some choose to use weapons and power to control and abuse others. You must never use either for that purpose, for with power comes the responsibility to provide guidance and protection to those who need it." Then he would instruct the boys on the finer techniques of swordplay and the use of the bow.

The boys marveled at the expertise that Mas demonstrated in the use of these weapons. During instruction, his movements with the sword were so effortless that it seemed the sword was an extension of his arm. Each movement blended into the next, a blur of fury and skill. With the bow, the boys would challenge him on a daily basis. They threw multiple targets into the sky to see if he could hit them before they fell to the ground. Each time the challenge was met. The elf was so quick and accurate that they thought it must be some sort of trick, but to Mas's abilities, there were no tricks. He was an efficient teacher, and the boys were excellent students, learning quickly.

As the boys' training progressed, Mas would cover their eyes and make them train without the benefit of sight. Sam excelled at the use of the bow, while Mas was completely amazed at how adept and skillful Jeff became with the sword. Soon the boys were proficient with or without their sight. Mas was relieved because he knew the day would soon come when his young charges would need those skills.

Finally, the terrain started to change, becoming very barren and dry, similar to places the boys had seen while traveling in the western part of their own country. Everywhere they looked, the land was strewn with small stones and large boulders. With all of the rocks, they had to be careful where they directed the horses. If one of the horses came up lame, it would slow their travel and they could ill afford any delays.

"What is the name of this place?" Jeff asked.

"It is called the Great Rock Plain," Mas said. "It is the door to the lands in the North."

Looking up into the sky, Sam half-expected to see a vulture circling overhead, waiting for its prey to perish from lack of water, when he noticed something flying toward them from the East. At first, the creatures looked like dots in the sky, but as they got closer, they appeared larger and more sinister.

"Mas, what are those things flying toward us?" Sam asked.

Mas had been preoccupied, thinking of the trails that he would have to navigate during the next few days, and didn't notice the creatures coming toward them. "What did you say?"

"There," Sam said pointing. "What are they?"

Mas looked up in alarm. "Quickly, follow me," Mas told the boys as he urged his horse toward a stony outcrop.

"Lay the horses flat and cover them with these blankets, and then conceal yourself amongst the rocks."

"What are we hiding from?" Sam whispered.

"Those creatures are called Ozlums," Mas said. "They roam the skies conveying what they see back to their masters, the Desert Boitus."

"What's a Desert Boitu?" Jeff asked.

"They are vile beings that have inhabited this land for as long as anyone remembers. Their hearts are as cold as the ice that covers the Northern mountains. They spread their misery like the winds spread the sands of the desert, slowly marching forward, laying waste to whatever stands before them. They work tirelessly to prevent a cure for our world's decay." Mas stopped. "Can you hear that?"

The boys listened and heard something on the wind, like huge wings beating a path through the sky and heading directly toward them. After a minute, they couldn't mistake the sound of the creatures landing. It was the same sound as when the flocks of geese landed in the fields that surrounded their home, only louder. And with all the rocks, the creatures were invisible to them.

"Are they close?" Jeff whispered.

Mas tapped his nose, and the boys understood why when a putrid odor filled their nostrils.

"That smells like the mouse that died in our basement," Sam said.

The odor was so bad the boys covered their noses with their sleeves. As the smell got even stronger, the horses became agitated, and Mas whispered something to them to quiet their uneasiness.

Mas and the boys could hear the Ozlums moving as their claw-like feet rasped over the boulders. Mas knew they were getting very close, so he motioned to the boys to get ready with their bows. They each grabbed an arrow. Mas had his bow in hand and had already notched a projectile when suddenly a noise like a thousand birds taking flight surprised them all.

Looking up, they could see many of the Ozlums flying to the East. The three pulled back, huddled next to the rocks, and listened. Then there was silence.

"Mas, I'm scared," Sam said. "What are these creatures going to do?"

"Shhh," Mas whispered.

"We'll be alright, we have Mas with us," Jeff mouthed to his brother.

Mas knew that the reek of the creatures could leave a disgusting odor for hours. In his head, he tried to calculate how many creatures had flown toward them and how many had flown away. He had a nagging feeling deep in his gut that the entire flock had not left.

"Are they still here?" Sam whispered.

Mas put his finger to his lips to keep Sam silent. After what seemed an eternity, the stench lessened but still wasn't completely gone, so the possibility of the creatures waiting in ambush remained. The Ozlums were very devious and had the patience of a hunter when it came to stalking their prey.

When the odor didn't disappear, Mas knew something was amiss. Slowly, he raised his head from behind the rocks. "I'm going to try to get a better view," he whispered. Moments later, Mas saw two enormous shadows cast onto the ground next to the boys. "We have been discovered!" he yelled.

CHAPTER EIGHT
The Boitus

The two creatures leapt to the ground from their overhead perch, and three more Ozlums rounded the outer part of the rock to confront Mas and the boys.

"Watch out for their wings! They use them as weapons!" Mas bellowed.

Jeff and Sam gasped at the sight of the Ozlums. They looked like huge, newly born birds as tall as men, all gray and pink with feathers that clung loosely to their drooping skin. Their beaked heads were large compared to their bodies, and they had big, sharp claws on their feet and smaller ones along the front of their massive wings. If it weren't for the size of the wings, one could wonder how they lifted themselves into the sky.

Mas let fly an arrow, piercing the throat of the largest Ozlum, but the second one was on him before he was able to prepare for another shot. The talons of the creature punctured Mas's outer garment, but didn't penetrate deep enough to do any physical harm. This gave Mas enough time to grab his sword and stab deep into the Ozlum's chest, slicing through its heart and ending its life.

The horses instantly took a position in front of the boys. They reared up and then stamped a threatening warning to the creatures to stay away. The Ozlums hissed at them and advanced toward the group.

Since they'd never really had to protect themselves from anything, much less such vile creatures as these, the boys' nervousness showed. They each released their first shots, striking the Ozlums in the wings but not slowing their momentum. The boys ran around the rock to get more arrows from their packs, while the horses kept two of the creatures engaged.

But before Jeff and Sam could grab the arrows, the third Ozlum landed in front of them. The creature hissed and jabbed at them with its steely beak. The boys separated and pulled their swords from their belts. The Ozlum came at Jeff, swinging its huge wings. Jeff barely avoided the sharp talons, but he was pushed backward toward some rocks. He slipped and fell, his sword flying from his hand. Immediately, the creature leapt into the air and pounced on Jeff, landing on his chest. The heavy blow knocked the breath out of Jeff, and he gasped for air. Now that the Ozlum had him trapped beneath its talons, it reared its head back, ready to sink its hardened beak into him.

At the terrible sight of his brother being hurt, Sam did the only thing that came to his mind. He hurled his sword at the Ozlum and, as it sunk into the creature's back, it let out a piercing scream and momentarily stopped the attack on Jeff. But the sword had only penetrated deep enough to distract the Ozlum. As the beast turned toward Sam, the sword fell from its back and landed next to Jeff. Although he was still being held captive, Jeff was able to grab his sword. He thrust it upward into the belly of the creature, slicing through the most vital organs and killing it.

The boys were almost in a state of shock at everything that had just happened, but they managed to quickly grab their bows and race to meet Mas. Lying near the horses were two Ozlums with arrows embedded deep in their bodies.

"Hurry, follow me!" Mas yelled.

They ran around the rocks as four more creatures took flight. They were very powerful flyers and would soon be out of range. Mas had already let fly one arrow, piercing the heart of the furthest Ozlum, but the other three were still close enough for a bow shot. Jeff and Sam both released arrows that struck the wings of the creature flying to the East. The other two screamed out their violent cries and flew in opposite directions, but not before Mas was able to get off one more shot, slicing into the wing of the largest creature.

With the Ozlums now out of arrow range, Mas reached into his pocket, pulled out a whistle, and blew into it. Within seconds, the eagle Windsong appeared, diving from above, focusing his attention on the Ozlum flying to the South. Because Mas's arrow had sliced deeply into the wing, slowing the flight of the largest creature, the eagle was able to catch it and complete what Mas had started. The eagle's talons dug deep, and soon a second Ozlum's body crashed to the desert floor.

Regrettably, the creature that Jeff and Sam had struck continued its flight to the East. If it made the full journey, the Boitus would soon know that someone or something was traveling through their lands.

"Now quickly, get the horses and let's get out of here," Mas said. He pointed to the distant hills. "We have to reach those foothills by nightfall."

By the end of the day, they had reached a stony outcrop that would lead them through a maze of canyons, then to the Great Wood, and finally to the mountains where they would face their fate.

"Mas, could we have a fire tonight?" Sam asked. The cold was settling into the boys' bones, and they wondered whether they would ever be warm again.

Mas shook his head. "Not tonight. Tonight, we will sleep with one eye open and the other one looking into the desert. Our presence is known, and we must be wary. It won't take long before the Boitus are on our trail. They travel fast and with purpose. If we're lucky, we will have until the morning. If not, we will have visitors this very evening. Besides, we are at the edge of the Garish region."

"Aren't those the Wild Elves?" Jeff asked.

"Yes, and I said I would tell you of my encounter, so I guess that time is now. Many years ago, when I was traveling through these canyons, I saved a young elf boy, but in doing so, I almost lost my own life. As soon as I had entered the canyons, I felt I was being watched. When I turned to find out who was watching me, I saw the boy on top of a crevice."

"How old was he? Was he all by himself?" Sam asked.

"I don't know his age and there was no one else with him," Mas said. "However, I must have startled him. When he tried to leave, the rocks under his feet broke apart and he fell. I could see that he'd grabbed onto a rocky ledge that opened to a deep fissure. If he fell, he would surely die."

"How high was he? Did he end up falling?" Sam asked.

"Listen, and I will finish. Knowing that he couldn't hold on for long, I climbed as fast as I could, and just as he fell, I grabbed his arm and pulled him to safety. During his tumble, he got a cut across his left eye that extended to his nose. When I finally set him down, he told me his name was Yuma. He was the son of the High Chief. I told him my name and then I bandaged his cut."

"How bad was his cut?" Sam asked. "Was he bleeding badly? I once fell and cut my knee and it bled a lot. I don't like to get cut."

"Sam, let Mas finish the story," Jeff said.

"After that, Yuma bowed to me, then scurried off into the valley. When I was heading back down to reach my horse and complete my travels, the rocks beneath my feet let loose and I tumbled down. I must have lost consciousness, for when I woke, I was in the Garish's dwelling. I was in pain, but their healer restored me to health. I stayed with the Garish for a few more days, and when I was well enough to leave, they blindfolded me and brought me back to the canyons where I resumed my travels."

"Why did they blindfold you?" Jeff asked.

"They didn't want me to know where the entrance to their canyon dwelling was. Only members of their tribe are allowed to know that. It was the last time I ever saw Yuma or any of his people. Maybe they will remember me and let us pass safely, but then again, maybe not. We must take precautions, and one of them is not to light a fire. We will eat a cold dinner tonight."

When they'd finished their meal, they bedded the horses down and prepared for a sleepless night. The weather that had plagued them since the beginning of their journey was being pushed southeastward by a light breeze coming out of the North. With the clouds gone, the two almost full moons lit up the valley below. From where they camped, they had a full view of anyone or anything approaching, human or otherwise.

"You two try to get some sleep," Mas told the boys. "I'll take the first watch." Mas had pushed them hard over the last few days and he knew they needed a rest, for the toughest part of their journey was just beginning. Before Mas had even reached his position overlooking the valley, the boys were sound asleep.

Mas sat on a large boulder observing the valley below. For the first few hours, all he could see were a few small creatures sniffing and foraging for anything edible, but unfortunately, for all their efforts, there was little gain. A few birds flew across the sky seeking a resting place or a light meal.

The night wore on and little happened. Clouds passed slowly by the moons, casting eerie shadows across the ground below. A light wind pushed air through the rocks, creating ghostly sounds. The hard riding of the last few days also weighed heavily on Mas. He was exhausted and his eyes became heavy, his chin bobbed to his chest more than once, and soon he too fell asleep.

He was awakened shortly after by Jeff shaking him and pulling him behind a large boulder. Jeff gestured for him to keep quiet.

"I couldn't sleep, so I came out to relieve you when I saw something moving below," Jeff whispered, pointing to a spot close to the valley floor.

At first, Mas couldn't see what Jeff was pointing to, but as his eyes adjusted to the glow of the night, he could make out four cloaked beings slowly moving below them. They were dressed in flowing robes and their heads were covered in hoods. They crept along silently and seemed to be following a scent along the rocky trail. Suddenly, they began to make clicking noises.

"What is that noise?" Jeff asked.

"I am sure it is the way they communicate with each other," Mas said.

Even from this distance, Mas knew who they were. The Ozlums had found their masters, the Boitus, and had let them know that intruders had entered their territory.

From between a split in the boulder, Jeff and Mas could see the approaching strangers. Sniffing the air, the largest of the Boitus looked in their direction. Instinctively, Mas and Jeff slipped further back behind the rocks. After a few minutes had passed, Mas peered out to see if they had been discovered. But the creatures seemed to have continued their search. Thankful that their hiding place had not been revealed, Mas and Jeff decided to go wake Sam and prepare to leave as soon as the time warranted.

But before they could reach him, Sam walked toward them. Both Mas and Jeff motioned for him to be silent and to crouch down behind the rocks. They pointed to the strangers below.

Sam took up position behind the boulder with Mas and Jeff. "What are they?" Sam whispered.

"They are the Boitus, the masters of the Ozlums that we saw this afternoon," Mas told him. "Let's go back to camp. They will most likely be here by dawn and we must be prepared to leave quickly."

"Why don't we leave now and be done with it?" Jeff asked.

Mas shook his head. "The valley is on the other side of this ridge. Even on the brightest of days, the path that we are going to travel will be full of peril and difficult to follow. It would not be wise to journey through there without all the advantages of daylight."

After saddling the horses and packing up their camp, the three returned to their lookout. The Boitus were still some distance away. The hooded figures moved slowly and deliberately, seeking every clue as to what they were following. Suddenly, as if on cue, they all stopped. The largest of them let out a hideous scream. The boys covered their ears as the sound pierced the night. When they thought that they could not take it a second longer, the creature became silent.

"What was that?" Sam asked.

"I am not sure, but I would say that it was some kind of call or summons for others to join them in the search. They seem to have slowed their ascent. I think they are waiting, but for what exactly, I don't know. I'm sure we will find out soon enough."

Soon they could see that the Boitus were settling down for the remainder of the night, and this allowed the trio to be a little more at ease, but no less vigilant.

"You stay here," Mas told the boys. "I'm going to set a little surprise for them. It may slow them down and put a little more distance between us."

When Mas returned, he was breathing hard and very sweaty. Sam, always the curious one, asked what kind of surprise he had set for the Boitus.

"Well, the only path to our location is through the narrow trail that we came up. If they try to get here any other way, they will have to climb over all sorts of rocks, which is not an easy climb, and it will surely delay them. Near the top of the trail, there is a stone that they must step on, and when they do, a small avalanche of rocks and boulders will come crashing down on them from above."

"Will it block the trail?" Jeff asked.

"It will either block the trail or send them running down to the bottom. Either way, it will delay them," Mas said.

Jeff and Sam spent the rest of the night listening to Mas tell more stories of how beautiful this world was prior to its devastation. They couldn't believe how quickly a land could be destroyed by so few people.

"Well, it's almost dawn and we should get going," Mas finally said.

"How far are the canyons from here?" Jeff asked.

"We are only a short distance away from them now. The entrance is down this steep, narrow path. We will be there shortly after sunrise."

The group trudged down the path, but when they turned to watch the sunrise, a movement in the East caught Jeff's attention.

"What's that?" Jeff said, pointing toward the far end of the valley.

Looking eastward, they could see a dust cloud moving over the low-lying hills.

"It's still too dark and I can't see clearly," Mas said, "but whatever it is, it's moving fast. Look how quickly the cloud travels over the rise."

"Maybe it's just a dust storm," Sam said.

"I don't think so," Mas said, concentrating on the movement of the cloud.

As the full light of dawn washed away the darkness, the mystery hidden by the night was revealed: a large band of riders with flowing robes were pushing their horses ever faster, ever forward.

"The Boitus come," Mas said. "We have to get out of here!"

CHAPTER NINE
The Canyons

Before the Boitus had arrived to meet their scouting group, Mas and the boys were well on their way into the canyons. Hopefully, the little surprise that Mas had left would slow their ascent and give them precious time to distance themselves from their pursuers.

"It's been years since I have traveled through the maze of canyons," Mas said.

Two huge rock pillars guarded the entrance. Each one

was carved, top to bottom, with beautiful animal features. Some were recognizable, while others were odd and unfamiliar.

"Look at the top of the carvings. What do you see?" Mas asked.

"It looks like a dragon's head," Sam said.

"That's correct. No one knows who did these carvings, or why. Maybe it was a warning to those who passed through the canyons, heading to the North country, for that is where the dragon lives."

"Those are amazing," Sam said. "I can't believe the detail of the carvings. I love to draw but I don't think I could do that out of rock."

"Yes, the artisans who carved these impressions must have been skilled beyond comparison," Mas said. "You can still make out the rings that lined the horns of the goats that lived along the canyon walls. It's incredible. Other than this access, the only other way into or out of the canyons that anyone knows of is the outlet into the Great Wood."

"Are there people living in the North?" Jeff asked.

Mas shook his head. "I don't believe so. The lands to the North are all barren. There were a few small settlements, but as our world dies, so do the villages."

"It would have been nice to go to one of those villages," Sam said. "Maybe they would have given us a hot meal."

"I have to agree, that would have been very nice," Jeff said.

"Beyond the Great Wood, there is the Northern Sea, where another land exists," Mas told the boys. "It is called Anwan. Word has spread that their lands are also faced with dire conditions."

"Do you think that Princess Iris will be able to help them?" Jeff asked.

"There is hope that she will save our whole world," Mas said. "Even though, at one time, the people of Anwan were Alfham's enemy. The Anwans are a fierce and ruthless race. They would travel across the Northern Sea and use this canyon pathway as a shortcut to raid the South. The shortcut would knock weeks off their journey and save precious supplies. In the days of constant marauding, the trails were so worn that no effort was needed to follow them. Finally, the old King of the South placed outposts all along the Northern Sea and through the forest path. This stopped the Anwans from invading our lands, and as things go, time and nature have a way of bringing the land back to its original condition. The natural elements of wind and rain erased any indications that a trail ever existed. Now, the only thing that allows one to pass through the canyons is luck or a great memory. For one wrong turn—and there are many—a traveler's bones may spend eternity as part of the landscape. Thankfully, I traveled through these canyons in my younger days so many times that I know almost every twist and turn."

Mas knew that with their head start, they should be able to reach the other side of the canyons before the Boitus had a chance to overtake them. Just maybe, the Garish would delay the Boitus's passage—he could only hope. Any delays that Mas and the boys encountered would surely cause problems because the hunters who were tracking them would not miss a trail. They hunted by scent, and that was one thing that Mas and the boys could not conceal.

"How long will it take us to get to the other side, Mas?" Sam asked.

"It takes a full day of constant traveling, and as long as we don't make any wrong turns, we should make it out by nightfall."

The sun had been baking the rock walls of the canyon all morning, and by noon, the heat had settled in the lower levels of the canyon, which made traveling more difficult.

Mas pointed up the trail. "Just ahead there should be a small pool under a rock overhang. The water comes from deep within the rocks. It is clean and cool. The horses need water, and we need to replenish our water bags. We could also use a quick break."

Soon, they reached the watering hole, where they identified the tracks of small animals and what appeared to be some scratched-out human prints. They watered the horses, refilled the water bags, and then sat down for a quick bite to eat.

Sam opened his pouch and let Cerith out to roam. "You must be getting awfully hungry," Sam told the ferret.

Except for her head occasionally peering through the opening in Sam's leather bag, Cerith had slept for most of the trip. They all watched her scamper and sniff through the little crevices and rocks, and soon enough, she caught a small rodent in her mouth and went off to find a nice shady spot to enjoy her meal.

"We should get going," Mas finally said to the boys.

They gathered their belongings and Sam put Cerith back in his bag. Then they resumed their trek through the canyon's maze. For the next few hours, they traveled in silence, each of them lost in their own thoughts as they gazed at the barren rock walls rising to meet the sky.

Jeff finally broke the silence. "Mas, how could anyone stay alive here, and what would they eat?"

"The people who live here have occupied these valleys for many years. No one really knows how they survive or how many live here. The belief is that they have a pretty active culture. I guess they have worked it out with nature."

The shadows along the canyon walls started to get longer, and they could feel the cold sliding down the sides of the surrounding stone barricades. The sun's warmth was leaving. Late afternoon was upon them.

"How much longer before we make it to the end?" Sam asked.

"It's not much longer now," Mas said. "If all goes well, we should make it out shortly after sunset."

Suddenly, a titanic sound of thunder rolled down the valley and, within seconds, a blast of air hit them.

"What was that?" Jeff asked, alarmed.

"It sounded like a rockfall, and it was close," Mas said. "Small rockfalls happen all the time, but this one was large, and that is why you have to constantly watch and listen for the slightest changes. It could mean the difference between life and death. If you pay attention, you will survive these gorges."

Rounding a turn in the canyon, they came upon a fork in the trail. A cloud of dust hung over everything. Huge boulders blocked the main trail, making it impassable for the horses.

"It looks like we've discovered the answer to the thunder," Mas said.

"Was that the way out of here?" Jeff asked.

"It was," Mas said

"What should we do?" Sam asked.

"Well, we have two options. We could release the horses, take the supplies, and trek over these boulders. Then we'd have to walk the rest of the way. But I fear that would consume precious time, and time is something we do not have.

More importantly, without the horses, I am afraid that this trek would be impossible to complete. For even if we succeed in our task, it would take us too long to walk back."

"I wouldn't want to leave the horses. How would they get home?" Sam asked.

"They would find their way," Mas said, "but what is pursuing us might hinder their passage."

"Then what should we do?" Jeff asked.

"I have heard that there is a third passage that leads out of the canyons," Mas told the boys. "The only problem is that no one has ever found it, or at least lived to talk about it. But there is a short verse that I remember from my first travels through these valleys and the secret may lie in its meaning. Sometimes, I think that it may have been made up to give those who were lost within the canyon walls some hope. Anyway, it goes like this:

Those of purpose will find a way when walls of stone keep them at bay.

Out of the darkest night, walls of stone rise to meet the moon's full light.

Then the day shall appear, so use it wisely for danger is near.

The given gifts will show a trace, a door that hides its outlined face

To give one passage to a protected place.

After Mas recited the verse, he looked at the boys and said, "Maybe we will get lucky and find that passage." Then he urged his horse down the trail to the right.

After a short time, the boys noticed Mas scanning the upper walls. He turned to them and said, "We have company."

Jeff and Sam scanned the high ground, trying to catch a glimpse of movement among the rocks. However, the only things they could see were high, puffy clouds advancing eastward and a large bird soaring high on the uplifting currents of air.

"Who is it?" Sam asked.

"The Garish," Mas said. "They're the dwellers of this land, and they are watching from behind the rocks. They've been with us since we took the split in the trail. They don't want to be seen, but when they do, they will show themselves. They haven't bothered us yet, so they are probably trying to figure out why we are here. Just look forward and keep going."

It was the first time that Mas had passed through these trails. They were much like the others, with rocks strewn about, walls of stone leading to the sky, and no signs of life anywhere.

"I wonder where we are," Sam said.

"I am not sure, but I think that it's time we call in some help," Mas said, gazing skyward.

The boys looked at each other, wondering what type of help they could get in this barren place. Mas reached into one of his pockets and pulled out the same whistle he had used to hail the eagle. He blew into it and soon they heard a screeching cry from above and saw a large bird diving toward them. Mas held his arm at a right angle high above his head, and Windsong soared past them and landed on his arm.

Mas turned to the eagle and emitted a series of high-pitched sounds. Windsong immediately flew from Mas's arm and ascended skyward. Soon he was doing lazy circles high above them.

Mas smiled. "Well, we have our beacon. All we have to do is follow the eagle."

Jeff loved knowing the names of birds and the calls that they made, so he asked Mas what the sounds he'd made to the eagle were.

"Long ago, humans and animals coexisted with each other on an extremely different level," Mas explained. "We communicated with each other through an ancient language. Then man created shelters, stopped living in the wild, and soon lost interest in understanding nature. Shortly after that, the language was lost to most. Some cultures kept the ability to speak to animals and, fortunately, mine was one of them."

"Can you teach us?" the boys asked in unison.

"If you wish. However, it will have to wait for another day, for we must be on our way. The ancient language definitely isn't something that can be learned in a few days."

They had come to another crossroad when Mas noticed that the eagle was soaring higher and higher.

"Something is wrong. Windsong can't find a path for us to follow. All of the paths ahead must be blocked." Then he spotted a plume of dust floating skyward. "Quickly, follow me," Mas commanded as he urged his horse forward.

Their horses carried them swiftly through the rough terrain, with some paths only wide enough for two horses to pass side by side. The twists and turns through the canyon were too numerous to count. But just when they thought the trail would never end, it emptied into a large open area that was surrounded by high rock walls.

"This reminds me of a sports stadium," Jeff said.

Mas looked at him, confused. "What's a sports stadium?"

"It's a large area surrounded by high walls where people watch teams compete with each other," Jeff said. "There is usually only one major way in and out of the stadium, and a few smaller exits located at the opposite end."

Mas nodded. "Ah, yes, that is very much our predicament. Hopefully, we will be able to find one of those ways out."

As they rode, they kept searching for the trail that would carry them out of the canyon. Mas saw that a section of the canyon narrowed toward the far end. Hoping there was an exit that way, they headed in that direction. But when they reached the end, they were greeted by a rock face that rose straight to the top of the canyon.

Mas immediately turned his horse around. "Quickly, we must go back, otherwise we will be trapped."

Driving their horses back to the entrance, the three noticed the dust cloud moving rapidly toward them. Mas put up his hand to stop everyone from moving. Suddenly, they could hear the distant echoes of many horses bouncing off the walls of the canyons. Their escape was blocked.

Mas pointed to Windsong up in the sky, then yelled as he turned his horse back into the bowl, "Follow me! We must hide!"

Mas and the boys galloped toward the far right-hand side of the canyon. When they stopped, the boys looked at each other, wondering how they were going to conceal themselves and the animals. Other than a slight swelling in the rock wall, it appeared to be sheer stone that reached up to the sky.

"How is this going to protect us?" Jeff asked urgently. "There is nothing here but a wall!"

"Dismount from your horses and follow me—and be quick about it," Mas told them.

As the boys dismounted, they looked at each other warily. Was Mas making the right judgment on their hiding spot? Then as they turned to follow him, he was gone.

"Where did he go?" Sam asked Jeff.

"I don't know, but he was just there. Mas, where are you?" Jeff called out.

Unexpectedly, they heard the elf's voice. It seemed to be coming out of the rock wall directly in front of them.

"We can't see you," Sam called back.

"I know, follow my voice."

The boys did what Mas told them. When they reached the rock, they put their hands out to prevent themselves from crashing into the wall, but to their amazement, they passed between the two sheer cuts of stone. The edges of the stone were so precise and well-matched that it couldn't even be recognized as an opening. The path traveled all the way to the top of the canyon and was only wide enough for a traveler and his horse to pass.

Jeff and Sam immediately spied Mas sitting on his horse, waving his arm, urging them forward.

"What was that?" Sam asked.

"They are called veil doors," Mas said. "They are made to conceal an entrance by using the natural surroundings."

Jeff looked puzzled. "I thought you said you'd never been here."

"I haven't."

"Then how did you know about the door?" Jeff asked.

"I saw Windsong fly that way. I assumed that it led to something—I just wasn't sure what. I can only hope that those coming for us will not find this passage. But I dare say, I believe the Boitus's sense of smell will lead them directly to us. Let's go!"

CHAPTER TEN
Moonlight

The beginning of the trail was narrow, and the walls reached high into the sky. Only a small amount of daylight was able to filter down to the bottom of the canyon. It made for very slow going, and the boys were starting to feel a little anxious.

"How long are we going to be in this ravine?" Jeff asked, even though he realized that Mas might not know the answer.

"I am not sure," Mas said, "but if you concentrate, you will smell something other than stone and dirt. We are close to the edge of the forest, but at this point, it may as well be across the sea because this wall of stone prevents our passage. Unfortunately, our choices are limited, and we must continue on this path until we find its end. I am afraid that if we go back, the Boitus will be waiting for us. But maybe, just maybe, we have been lucky enough to have discovered the entrance into the Garishes' Keep."

"What is the Garishes' Keep?" Sam asked.

"It is not a what, but a place," Mas explained. "It is where the Garish people live. As I said, the old King placed outposts all through the land to stop the raiders. When the raiding ceased, most people returned to their homes in the South. However, some of them stayed and created a new life in this barren and desolate land. Those people are called the Garish."

"They're the ones who saved you," Sam said.

Mas nodded. "Yes, they are."

"How can they live here?" Jeff asked. "There isn't anything to eat, and it seems there's very little to drink."

"It is said that they have developed and set up a thriving culture," Mas said. "They have been here for ages, so I am sure they have figured out a way to survive."

The trail started to widen and soon it emptied into a small open area, but as they looked around, their hearts sank. They were trapped. There was no way out. The walls of the canyon shot straight up to the sky. The rock face was so smooth that not even the most accomplished rock climber could gain a foothold. Lastly, there was no door.

"Mas, what are we going to do? We're trapped," Jeff said.

Sam grabbed Jeff's arm, looking very worried. "Are we going to be okay?"

"Never, ever give up hope," Mas told the boys. "Today's problem is tomorrow's memory. Let's see what we have to work with." He urged his horse onward.

But as they reached the end of the ravine, they realized that it was hook-shaped and protected enough to give them shelter from the creatures hunting them. Unfortunately, that would only be for as long as the food and water lasted. There was no going back. Unless the Garish liberated them from their current predicament, Mas knew that this was where they would have to make their stand against the Boitus. He knew these creatures would eventually find the entrance that would lead them to this spot, but he decided the boys didn't need to know that—at least for now.

"As much as I would like to have a cooked meal, I don't think it would be a good idea to have a fire," Mas cautioned. "The Boitus would catch the scent of smoke and we don't want to give them any help in finding us."

The boys agreed, although their obvious disappointment showed on their faces.

"I have a great idea," Mas said, knowing he had to cheer the boys up. "I've been saving this for a special time, and since we need a hot meal and we can't have one, I'd say the time has come."

He reached into his saddlebag and pulled out a packet wrapped in thin leather. It was the size of a small loaf of bread and Mas treated it as if it were gold. "This bread is a great indulgence in my land. From the day one starts to make it, it takes a full turn of the moon before it is ready to eat. It will nourish our bodies with enough energy for days of hard travel, and there is nothing that satisfies my taste buds like this."

Mas opened the packet and broke off a piece of bread for each boy. Sam and Jeff sat down, each taking a bite. As they chewed slowly, smiles as wide as a river spread across their faces.

"This tastes incredible," Jeff mumbled between bites.

The only thing that was said until the loaf of bread disappeared was Sam's satisfied moan of "Oh, this is so good!"

And so, with full bellies and something that warmed their bodies more than a hot fire, they were all ready to face the cold evening and whatever the night brought them.

Jeff sat on a large stone and Sam sat next to Mas, each in their own thoughts, staring at the only way in or out of the ravine, and not knowing what might emerge through the opening at any moment.

Mas knew that he needed to prepare the boys for what was coming. "Do you remember what I told you earlier about the two full moons?"

"Yeah," Jeff said. "You told us it would be so bright that it would shine like daylight."

"Well, tonight is the night it's going to happen," Mas said. "There isn't a cloud in the sky, so it is going to be tremendously bright. But because the ravine is so narrow, the light will not appear until the moons pass directly over us. Until then, darkness will invade this area like a horde of locusts. You will be lucky to see your hand in front of your face. We must be very quiet and listen for the slightest of sounds, for that will be the only indication that the Boitus have arrived. They are silent and cunning and will want to see if we have any defenses. They will first test us by sending a small party to see how prepared we are."

"I'm scared," Sam said.

Jeff looked at his brother. "Me too."

"Mas, if they get us, what will they do to us?" Sam asked.

Mas tried to reassure his young charges. "If I have anything to do with it, they aren't going to get you. You must be brave. This is where all your training will be tested. Remember your lessons."

"I didn't like shooting the Ozlums," Sam said. "I felt terrible. I don't want to shoot anything ever again."

"Sam, no one should ever take pleasure in killing or harming another living creature," Mas said. "However, sometimes it has to be done for your safety and the safety of the ones you love."

Sam and Jeff slowly nodded, knowing that Mas was right. As the night wore on, both boys were getting very sleepy.

"I wish we could go home," Sam said.

"I know, but we are here, and we have to finish what we started," Jeff said.

"I know," Sam said, but he didn't look happy about it. "I wonder if it's Christmas yet."

"No, I don't think so. Mas said we would be back before then."

"I hope the Boitus don't find us," Sam said.

Jeff put his arm around his brother. "So do I."

As the boys sat listening for any sound, their eyes started to get heavy and their heads slumped more than once, when suddenly a flurry of stones hit the ground all around them. Were the rocks dislodged by an unwelcome guest or had someone thrown them to the ground from above? Whatever it was, it immediately brought the boys awake and alert. They understood that the slightest movement, obscure sound, or subtle scent riding the wind could possibly mean the difference between living and dying.

"This must be what animals feel like when they're hunted," Jeff said to Mas.

Mas nodded in agreement, but more than that, he was proud of the boys' grasp of their situation. *They have grown,* he thought to himself. *Maybe we will get through this.*

A shaded light began to filter down into the canyon and soon they could see a sliver of the moon starting its short journey across the narrow ravine. They all knew what was coming next.

"Remember what I have taught you," Mas whispered. "Stay within yourselves. Shoot small and stay focused. Let your instincts be your guide."

As he turned his attention back to the opening, he detected three Boitus creeping along the far side of the rocks and another on the opposite side, all slowly inching their way toward their location.

Mas spoke softly. "They are here, but this is just a scouting group. They have come to test our strength."

He pointed the creatures out to Jeff and Sam. The boys were still hidden from view, but from their position they could easily see the whole area in front of them.

"Wait until you know that you have an accurate shot and then release," Mas told them as they each notched an arrow.

"Remember our lessons, remember our lessons," Sam and Jeff kept repeating under their breath.

Suddenly, the Boitus were upon them and arrows from all three bows released at the same time, each one striking a Boitu. No longer would any of these three creatures present a danger to this small band of travelers. But seeing their companions fall brought out the wrath in the Boitus. Five of them ran freely across the opening, toward the end of the ravine, where Mas and the boys stood. The first three fell easily as each one took an arrow to the chest. The largest creature reached Mas, but not before he was able to pull out his sword and deflect the powerful swing of the beast's curved blade. The other Boitu ran at Sam, but as it did, it slipped on the loose gravel, giving Sam time to notch another arrow and let it fly straight into the creature's heart.

Before long, Mas had put an end to his adversary, and all was quiet. It was so silent that they could hear one another breathe. The moons would soon be at their apex, and everything would show as clear as day.

But in all the chaos, they had missed the creature that had slunk to the far side of the ravine and was now within striking distance of the group. Jeff was facing Mas and Sam when Sam gasped. He tried to yell but no sound escaped his lips. Jeff saw the horror in his brother's eyes. He turned, drew his sword, and hurled it, pinning the last of the Boitus to the rock wall.

Then, echoing down the canyon walls were the horrible sounds of many more Boitus fast approaching.

"Quickly, get behind the rocks," Mas said.

Temporarily safe in their new position, they waited. The moons were directly overhead, and the light shone as brightly as a thousand candles. It pierced the darkness of the canyon, passing through the eye of the sword handle, revealing behind them a small opening in the rock wall.

Jeff was the first to notice. He pointed to an area behind Sam and Mas. They turned to see the outline of a door glowing on the rock wall.

All at once, it came to them. They looked at each other and yelled, "It's the verse!"

Those of purpose will find a way when walls of stone keep them at bay.

Out of the darkest night, walls of stone rise to meet the moon's full light.

Then the day shall appear, so use it wisely for danger is near.

The given gifts will show a trace, a door that hides its outlined face

To give one passage to a protected place.

They all ran to the wall and pushed on the door, but it wouldn't budge.

"Why won't it open?" Jeff shouted.

"Look where the moonlight shines. There is a keyhole," Mas bellowed.

At that moment, Sam remembered something. He ran to his horse and grabbed the small leather pouch, reached inside, and pulled out a key.

"This key was in the pouch that Azar gave me at the toy store," Sam said excitedly. "I think it was meant to open this door."

Suddenly, they heard loud screams reverberating through the ravine. The horrible noise sounded like thunder and madness all at once.

"Quickly, see if the key works," Mas urged. "The full attack will not happen until the light of the moons has passed, and that will be very soon." He looked at the sliver of moon starting to disappear over the far edge of the canyon.

Sam ran to the solid rock wall and placed the key into the hole. It fit perfectly! The wall began to shudder, and then an opening appeared. Inside was as dark as anything they had ever seen, but they knew it was their only chance for escape.

"I'm not leaving my sword," Jeff said, scrambling up the rocks and pulling it from the stone. He raced back to Sam and Mas.

"Hurry, we are losing the moonlight!" Mas yelled.

The small group of travelers quickly gathered all their belongings, rushed toward the door, and entered the unknown darkness. The last thing they heard was the scraping of rock and the screams of the many creatures trying to reach them— and then, silence.

CHAPTER ELEVEN
A New Escape

The silence was deafening. Even the animals were quiet and still, waiting to hear if they were in the company of someone or something worse than what they had just escaped. When time passed without incident, Mas whispered to the boys, "Stay silent for a while longer. You never know what may be lurking in the darkness."

"It's cold in here," Sam whispered to Jeff.

"I know, but it's better than being out there," Jeff said.

They kept looking around, hoping to get a glimpse

of something, but the darkness was so complete that the only way they knew they were all still together was by the sound of their breathing and the occasional thump of a horse's hoof against the rock floor.

As they waited, time seemed to stand still. *How long had they been standing there?*

"Mas, does it seem to be getting warmer in here?" Jeff said quietly.

"Yes, it does," Mas said. "We must be at the end of a small cave. With the animals and our body heat, the chill is leaving. Hold on for a few more minutes. I have to get something out of my pack."

Mas felt his way to his horse. He quickly found what he was looking for and pulled it from his pack. The boys could hear the unraveling of leather. Again, the silence came. But suddenly, they noticed a blue glow radiating from Mas's hands.

"What is that?" Sam asked.

"It is a small glow stone. I found it traveling through these canyons many years ago. One night, as I was sitting by the fire, I noticed a round object on the ground. When I picked it up, it started to glow, and the longer I held it, the brighter it became. It seems to radiate with heat."

No sooner had Mas spoken than the walls of the cave began to glow a similar bluish hue.

"Look at the walls!" Jeff said excitedly.

The walls were emitting enough light to cast shadows on their surroundings. Mas navigated his way to the wall to see what was creating the light. He noticed that there were many small blue stones embedded in the rock's surface. He blew his hot breath onto the stones and, to his delight, they emitted a bright blue glow.

"These stones are not natural to these walls," Mas told the boys. "It appears that someone has placed them here. See the sticky material behind the stones? It seems to be some sort of pitch that keeps the glow stones in place."

"Do you think it was the Garish?" Jeff asked.

"That would be my guess," Mas said.

"Why do you think they did that?" Sam asked.

"The stones react to the slightest temperature change," Mas explained. "I can only assume that someone embedded these stones to illuminate the passageways. If there are people living within these caves, the residue from constantly burning torches would foul the air and eventually make them ill. This way they keep their air clean and breathable. I wonder what other surprises we may discover before we depart."

It was now light enough for them to see their surroundings. They had entered the cavern at the end of a narrow passageway. A solid wall of rock blocked their travel in all but one direction. As they looked around, they noticed that even though the entrance to the cave was concealed on the outside, from the inside, the door was very visible.

It was a spherical cut in the wall. To open the door, there was a lever that released a large circular stone sandwiched between the outer and inner valley walls.

"It seems like we should have been able to see this door from the outside," Jeff said.

"I am sure the craftsmen that created this doorway were much more than stone carvers," Mas said. "There was some deeper magic involved here. What it is, we may never know. But look, the area around the door is well worn, which means it is used frequently."

"How do we get out of here?" Jeff asked.

"Well, on that side of the door we know what awaits us, so we can't go that way," Mas said.

Sam shuddered. "No, I don't ever want to see another Boitu."

"Then I guess there is only one way out of here," Mas said as he pointed down a dark tunnel.

"That looks kind of creepy," Jeff said.

"Hopefully, the glow stones will light our way," Mas reassured.

As they made their final preparations to leave, Sam noticed a small point of light at one end of the tunnel that was getting brighter. He tapped Mas on the shoulder and pointed in the direction of the light.

"Draw your blades quietly. Something comes this way," Mas whispered.

The boys did as they were told, and their heartbeats quickened in anticipation of what might be approaching. Soon they could hear footfalls echoing through the cavern—from the sound of it, a small army was headed their way.

"Do you think the Boitus found another entrance?" Sam asked nervously.

"No, I don't think so," Mas whispered. "Whoever travels this way knows that we are here. We are the intruders."

Before long, they could make out bodies moving within the wave of blue light, and they realized that the group approaching was much smaller than they had anticipated.

"Judging by what we heard, I thought there would be many more men than this," Jeff said.

"I'm sure they planned it that way," Mas said. "Put your weapons away. They mean us no harm."

"How can you be so sure?" Jeff asked.

"They carry very few weapons and there is no need to alarm them with our weapons drawn. If they meant to harm us, we would have encountered many more heavily armed men. I believe they have been expecting us."

As the group stopped in front of the trio, Mas recognized the man leading them. Yuma had grown since the last time they had met, but the scar he'd gotten when he fell all those years ago still crossed his left eye and stopped at the bridge of his nose. His body was solid like the rocks of his home. He stood tall over most of the others in his company.

Yuma looked at the boys and then at Mas. A smile lit up his face as he recognized the person standing in front of him. The two men took a step toward each other and embraced warmly. This show of affection released any tension among the men and put the boys at ease.

"I am Yuma, son of Eldarenth, our elder and leader," the man with the scar told the boys.

Yuma gestured to the men standing next to him, introducing them. "This is Helka, the fighter; Asku, the one who keeps watch; and Tanuka, the watcher of horses."

After Mas presented the boys to the group and gave a quick explanation of how they had fallen into their current predicament, Yuma and his men led the small troop toward their home.

"Yes, we know who seeks you," Yuma said. "We were the ones who threw rocks to wake you to the Boitus's presence."

"We thank you for that," Mas said.

"We will hear the rest of your story and why you are on this journey after you have rested your eyes," Yuma said.

As they walked, the tunnel became wider and wider, and the blue glow stones became more abundant. Soon the passageway was large enough for five men to walk side by side. The twists, turns, and openings within the cave were too numerous to count.

"Yuma, do you ever get lost? There are so many tunnels," Sam said.

Yuma laughed. "Like in life, there are many roads that a man can choose to walk. Some paths lead so far away that one may never return, but if your heart is where your home is, all paths lead home. Just follow your heart and you will never be lost."

They walked on for a while longer and then stopped at a split in the tunnel.

"Take what you need for the night," Yuma told them. "We are approaching the main living area and this is as far as the animals are allowed. Asku and Tanuka will make sure that your horses are well fed, watered, and bedded for their stay."

Sam thought of Cerith and pulled her out of his pack. "Yuma, could my friend stay with me?" Sam asked.

Yuma and his men smiled at the sight of the ferret.

"My friend, your companion would be most welcome in our home, for he may rid us of many small, unwelcome lodgers that roam our dwelling," Yuma said.

The group led the boys and Mas to an enormous cavern. It was still dark, and it was difficult to make out their surroundings. Shadows were cast throughout by a source of light emanating high above them. It was a single, muted glow, like someone putting a piece of cloth in front of a light bulb.

"What is that glow high above us?" Sam asked.

"It is the light of the two moons," Yuma said. "It is usually much darker in our home, but tonight the brightness of the moons allows us to see."

Jeff and Sam looked at each other, clearly wanting to ask more questions, but Mas gave them a wave of his hand, indicating that there would be no more questions for the night. The secret of the moons glowing within the cave would have to wait until the morning.

At the far side of the cavern, Yuma pushed open a door that was woven from straw and took Mas and the boys inside. The two other men went in a different direction.

"This is where you can spend the rest of the night," Yuma said. "Sleep as long as you require, for your journey has been trying and you must rest. I will see you in the morning. Then we will speak to my father and the elders to see if we can help you on your way."

The space was small but all around the outside walls were places to bed down. The boys took off their outerwear and lay down. Surprisingly, the beds were very soft and comfortable.

Mas ended his conversation with Yuma, and as he turned to say goodnight to the boys, he noticed they were already sound asleep.

"Sleep and rest, young masters, for your true trial is yet to come," Mas whispered.

CHAPTER TWELVE
New Companions

"How are we going to get past the dragon?" Sam asked Jeff.

So far, the fearsome beast had not noticed them crouched behind a large stone. They had to get to the other side, but how? Suddenly, the dragon turned toward them and sniffed *the air. It let out a tremendous roar and spewed a blast of fire toward their hiding spot. The flames did not reach them, but they could feel the heat. Now the dragon was coming closer. The next blast would cover them—they had to run. They both jumped up and, at that moment, it hit them. A blaze of fire so bright that they threw up their hands to protect their eyes, but for some reason, it didn't burn.*

Jeff and Sam both lowered their hands from their faces, and there was Mas, outlined in the door with a stream of light so bright they had to momentarily avert their eyes.

"Are you going to sleep the whole day away or do you want something to eat?" Mas asked.

"Eat!" the boys replied as they jumped out of bed.

Mas closed the door. As they were getting dressed, Sam told Jeff that he had just had the scariest dream. Jeff always listened to the tales of Sam's vivid dreams, for he had many, but this one held Jeff's attention more than usual. Sam told him of the mountain, the desolation of its surroundings, and the awful smells that penetrated every breath. But more than that, there was the monster that lay within the mountain. He told Jeff how they had to sneak through tiny hidden tunnels beneath the mountain to get around the dragon's lair, and then finally, the encounter with the beast.

Jeff stopped Sam and finished telling the rest of his dream for him.

Sam was amazed. "How did you know my dream?" Sam asked.

"We must have had the same dream!" Jeff said.

"That is so weird!" Sam exclaimed.

Jeff nodded his head in agreement, thinking how real the dream had seemed. How could they both have had the exact same dream? Deep down in the pit of his stomach, Jeff felt a little scared of this dream.

"We'd better get going before Mas comes after us again," Jeff said.

They opened the door and entered a very strange and unfamiliar dwelling. It was cavernous. They'd had no idea how large an area they had passed through last night.

Sam looked around. "Jeff, this is as big as our school's soccer field!"

"Bigger," Jeff said.

Remembering how they had seen the moon glowing within the cave, the boys looked up. What they saw was far more extraordinary than what they'd expected. The entire top side of the cave was a beautiful clear gemstone. A huge light could be seen on the other side of the crystal, bouncing rays of light off every surface and warming the rocks below to create a comfortable heat throughout the cavern.

"This reminds me of us being inside one of my large geodes," Jeff said. "But that glowing object is the sun!"

"I know," Sam said. "It's absolutely spectacular."

They noticed that channels were cut within the rocks around the outer edges of the cave. They could see water flowing into the top channel from an outside source, dripping over the edge and streaming into the channel below. This system was set up throughout the cavern. Each of the channels had plants in them, and most of them seemed to be bursting with some sort of fruits or vegetables. All the waterways finally emptied into a large basin at the bottom, where a number of people were filling containers with water.

"Look over there," Jeff said.

High along the wall of the cave, a young girl was suspended by a rope. She was cutting what appeared to be round red fruits from one of the channels and placing them into a basket that was tied to her waist.

"This must be one of the ways they get their food," Jeff said.

The boys were standing on the highest elevated path that went around the whole dwelling. From there, they had a view of the entire domicile. There were four large access points on the outside of the cavern walls—north, east, south, and west. From each, a wide path angled down to a large circular area at the base of the cavern, which, by the looks of the activity there, functioned as the central living space. Also, at different levels around the cavern, circular avenues were cut into the rock to form large, flat areas. The family dwellings seemed to be situated on the level where the boys stood. Many stone staircases were cut into the rock leading to each different level, allowing ease of movement throughout the whole space. It was an ingenious design. Every path gave great access to the center of the living area, but if you had to leave quickly, you could easily flee to safety through any of the four exits.

People filled the immense dwelling, all seeming to have a destination and purpose in mind. Some were tending small shops, none of which appeared to be locked. The boys saw people mending clothes, sharpening blades of steel, hanging plants to dry, and performing all sorts of daily activities. Children laughed and chased each other, bumping into adults who didn't seem to notice the annoyance.

At the bottom of the cavern, Jeff and Sam noticed a group of people gathered in the center. They could make out Mas sitting and speaking with several men and women.

"We should probably get down there," Jeff said. "They must be waiting for us."

The boys walked down one of the main avenues, observing all the activities. When they got close to the center, they could see that there were many waiting for their attendance. Other than Mas, Yuma, and the men they had met the night before, they didn't recognize anyone.

When they finally reached the group, Yuma stood up to make the introductions. Jeff and Sam listened attentively as they stood next to Mas.

"This is Alina," Yuma said. "She is my wife as well as the best bowman in all the land. Her name means 'warrior spirit.' There is no one finer in the skill of the bow or the knife."

Alina nodded in thanks for the recognition of her great skills. She had long, dark hair that hung in braids below her waist. She was almost as tall as Yuma, and her skin was light brown. Alina was a beautiful woman, and she had a look of intelligence and strength. A knife was strapped to her waist and a bow and quiver of arrows hung from her shoulders.

Sam nudged Jeff in the ribs to prevent him from staring too long at Alina.

"This is my father, Eldarenth," Yuma continued. "He is our elder and he leads our people."

Eldarenth nodded to Mas, Jeff, and Sam. He was dressed similarly to Yuma, but he wore an intricately beaded wrap around his shoulders. Eldarenth was an enormous man. In his younger days, he was probably as tall as Yuma. He wasn't heavy; he was just massive. His eyes indicated knowledge and kindness, perfect for a leader. He too had a knife strapped to his waist.

Next to Eldarenth sat a woman who was holding his hand. She stood when Yuma introduced her.

"This is my mother, Ailen. My father would say that without her, ruling would be much more difficult," Yuma said.

"It is a pleasure to meet you," Ailen said to the boys. "You are so young to be on such a quest. May the Great One guide and protect you through these difficult times."

This time, it was Sam's turn to be mesmerized by the beauty of this woman. Her face was as smooth as glass, and her skin was as white as a glimmering opal. Her blond hair shone with light. She exuded purity and the wonders of the natural world. She too was almost as tall as Yuma. One could now see where Yuma had inherited his considerable size.

In the final introduction, Yuma walked over to an older woman and, as she stood, he gave her a hug, showing his love and respect.

"This is Eletha. She is the mother of Eldarenth. She is our spiritual leader, healer, and the person to whom many owe their lives," Yuma said.

"I am one of those," Mas said.

Eletha's hair was pure white. Her body had shriveled from age, with the wrinkles on her face as deep as the valleys the boys had passed through. But what really made an impression on them was how she was looking at them. The irises of her eyes were solid white, indicating that she might be blind. But even without being told, the boys knew that she was seeing deeply into their beings. It didn't make them uncomfortable, for there was something about her that radiated warmth, security, and great wisdom.

She looked at Jeff and Sam for a moment longer, and then finally spoke. "There is an ancient prophecy that tells of two young boys entering our world and making it possible for our land to heal. It is an undertaking that you alone must face, and it will be filled with many dangers. How you face these perils will not only determine if our world survives, but the type of person you will become."

"What's a prophecy?" Sam asked.

"It's when something is predicted to happen in the future," Jeff said.

Eletha continued. "You have been selected by something greater than man. Why, we do not know. It is a burden that ones so young should not be called upon to carry, but you have been chosen and, because of that, you must face what lies ahead of you. May the Great One guide and protect you."

Eldarenth stood. "Mas has told me where you must travel. My son and his wife will guide you through the Wood, for there are many unseen threats that lay in the bowels of this dark forest. Here, our world flourishes because we are good guardians, but as you saw through your travels, our world is slowly dying. Man has neglected our mother through greed and disregard for her. She needs mending. Hear our council and accept our gifts, for these may give you the wisdom and the advantage you may need to help you complete your task."

After Eldarenth had finished, Eletha stood again. For someone who looked to be old and frail, she stood with amazing quickness and agility. She walked up to the boys and took each of their hands within hers, looked them in the eye, and spoke.

"I have lived a long life and have seen many strange and wonderful things. There are many accounts of creatures that once inhabited our worlds. These stories are passed on by travelers such as yourselves. I can tell you this:

these stories are not myths, for in our world these beasts do exist. There are beings in this world who are kind and beautiful, yet there are others who are cruel and ugly."

"We have already seen Boitus and Ozlums," Sam said. "Are there creatures worse than these?"

"Much worse, and these creatures are living within the Wood that you must pass through to reach your final destination," Eletha said.

"Is there a way around it?" Jeff asked.

"Yes, but it would take many weeks to go around the Wood, and I believe that your time in our world is limited."

"What kind of beings could be worse than Boitus and Ozlums?" Sam asked.

"Boitus, Ozlums, and most creatures can be dealt with by man. But there is another being that roams the Wood who is not of the natural world," Eletha told them. "It exists somewhere between the physical world and the spiritual world."

"Should we be troubled about this creature?" Mas asked.

"You should be concerned and aware of everything that dwells within the woodland," Eletha cautioned. "This being is the master of the forest and he protects all that inhabit the Wood. If you can help it, do not harm anything as you pass through its domain. If you do, you may be visited by him."

"What is this creature called?" Mas asked.

"It is called the Leshy," Eletha said.

Mas clearly wanted to know more. "How can we protect ourselves against it?"

"Since the Leshy's world is so dark, it despises light. There are a few things that will give you short reprieves from the darkness. One is a glow stone, but again, it will only create a temporary barrier. The Leshy's magic is strong, and its power will eventually diminish the light of the glow stones. Once the stones' light is diminished, he will advance without fear."

Eletha handed each of the company a beautiful glow stone. "Keep this with you at all times, for you never know when you will need it."

"Is there anything else that we should know?" Yuma asked.

"Be aware of your animals' behavior," Eletha advised. "They are more sensitive to the spiritual world than we are, and they will know if he approaches. They will feel his presence, and their nervousness will show. If he is near, a darkness will appear, and it will advance toward you from every direction. Do not run, for you can't escape this blackness—it is complete. However, there is one other thing that may protect you."

Eletha reached into a woven basket and pulled out a leather pouch. She opened it and held up a beautiful stone.

It was about the size and shape of an egg. The colors were amazing. It shone with every color of the rainbow and all of them seemed to be moving within the stone while never reaching its surface.

Eletha handed the stone to Yuma, and, in turn, it was passed to Alina, Mas, and Sam. Finally, it was passed to Jeff. When Jeff touched it, the stone blazed with beautiful colors. It was warm to the touch and the warmth seemed to penetrate through his whole body. He stared at it for the briefest of moments, enchanted by its beauty. Just as he was about to speak, the stone suddenly turned cold, and all of the colors disappeared.

Eletha looked at Jeff. "This is the Crystal of Paladin and it appears to have chosen you as its keeper. Its light is very powerful against the spirit world. Did you feel the warmth pass through you as you held it?"

"Yes, it was a wonderful feeling," Jeff said.

"You are now bonded to the Crystal, and it will know when you need its power. When it is required, it will create a light that will suspend time. Once released, nothing can penetrate the light, not even the Leshy. The light gives those within its circle the ability to see what isn't normally visible. If confronted by the Leshy, you may be able to see into its soul and find a solution where once there was only hopelessness. But I warn you, only use the Crystal's power if all else fails. For if no solution is found, you may be locked into the circle of light for eternity."

Jeff nodded solemnly, trying to take in all that the wise woman had told him. He carefully placed the Crystal of Paladin back in its pouch. He knew he would have to carry it with him for the rest of the journey.

Mas hated to interrupt, but he finally said, "We must be on our way, for time is our enemy."

"Wait, there is one last gift I would like to give," Eletha said, pulling out a small leather bag. She handed it to Sam.

"What is this?" Sam asked. He opened it and found that it was filled with sand.

"There will come a time when everything seems lost and no path exists," Eletha told him. "Spread the sand before you and it will show you the way."

Both Jeff and Sam thanked Eletha for their gifts.

"Thank you for your generosity," Mas added. "You have been most gracious, but we must be on our way."

"Everything is ready to go," Yuma said. "The packs are full of stores and the water bags are filled. We leave after we have had our morning meal."

Jeff and Sam looked at each other. They knew the most important part of their journey was now beginning.

CHAPTER THIRTEEN
Into the Wood

It didn't take long after leaving the safety of the Garish dwelling that the troop was able to see the borders of the Wood. Since they were coming off a high plateau, they could see the Wood spread out before them like a blanket across the land. It would take a man on horseback weeks to travel around the forest, but since they were entering it from the narrowest part, they could cross it in two long days. It was immense and dark. From the high plateau, they could make out the mountainous area where their journey would come to its ultimate end.

As they walked along the trails that led to the Wood, each person was deep in thought as to what lay ahead. They all knew and understood that there would be many more obstacles they would encounter before reaching their destination. However, what lay at the end would be the most treacherous of all.

"Are you afraid?" Jeff asked Sam.

"A little. How about you?" Sam said.

"I think it's scary, but remember, we have Mas, Alina, and Yuma with us," Jeff said. "And don't forget what Mom and Dad always told us: when things get difficult, you just keep putting one foot in front of the other and eventually you will get to where you are going—and never give up. I guess that's what we must do."

Late in the afternoon, they arrived at the edge of the Wood and saw what looked like an ancient path. A stone arch stood supported by two moss-covered pillars, and a stone-paved road signaled the beginning of the Wood trail.

"It's a very old road," Yuma told the group. "You would never realize by looking at its current condition that it had once carried men to the Northern Seas to protect our lands from the Anwan raiders. During this time, the forest was beautiful and safe to cross. The King of the South built a great road through the narrowest part of the Wood to quicken travel for his armies. All along the road, he placed fortresses to aid his men as they passed."

"Will we see any of these fortresses? Maybe we can sleep in them," Sam said.

"I am sure that we will see them," Yuma said, "but they may be in such disrepair that we do not want to enter them, and one never knows what may be living inside."

Yuma stared into the dark forest. "It's evening and we should stop to rest the animals and get something to eat. We will proceed at first light. We need to spend as few nights as possible in the Wood, for this is no longer the beautiful forest it once was."

The path that led into the Wood was covered in brush and leaves. Large trees pushed through the stones that had once created a flat surface for wagons and men to travel on. Twisted branches tangled together blocked the path, giving warning to those who dared to enter that their travel through the forest would be difficult.

As they sat eating, Sam asked Yuma, "Why is it so quiet? I haven't seen any birds or small animals for a while. Where did they go?"

"This is a dark place and life exists in the shadows," Yuma explained. "Present yourself and you may be taken before it is your time. The forest creatures conceal themselves and stay well hidden—they remain unseen and that is what we will do. If we need to speak, we will whisper. When we eat, meals will be cold. We must become invisible during our passing and, if we are lucky, we will pass through to the other side like a silent breeze."

Daylight was fading into night and soon, without a fire, the chill of the night would penetrate even the warmest clothing. Jeff and Sam sat in silence, finishing their cold meals and straining to hear any sounds that would give them the slightest clues as to the creatures that lay ahead.

Finally, Mas stood and spoke to the boys. "I think it is time that we get some sleep, for there will be little of that over the next two days. Dress warmly. There is a particular chill in the air tonight."

Jeff and Sam huddled close to each other for warmth. With the thought of entering the forest the next morning hanging over them, they knew they would get little sleep that night. Each had a sense of foreboding about entering the Wood. It was menacing enough to be looking at it from the outside, but what would the inside bring? They lay in silent thought, neither of them speaking. Finally, out of sheer exhaustion, they fell into a fitful sleep. Visions of monsters chasing them through the forest plagued their dreams.

* * *

The boys woke with a start. They looked at each other and then at the Wood. The silence they had encountered since they arrived had been replaced by a slow, menacing hum. They could see that Mas and the others had moved close to the edge of the forest to try to understand what they were hearing.

Suddenly, Yuma turned to the boys and told them to gather their belongings and move the horses behind some large rocks that bordered the Wood.

As soon as they had ducked behind the rocks, the hum turned into a deafening roar. Something was approaching, crashing through the forest, not letting anything stand in its way. Small trees and branches were tossed through the air. The boys kept down as debris landed all around them. The sound became so piercing that they had to cover their ears, and just when they thought they couldn't stand it any longer, it stopped—and then, nothing.

Except for the occasional thump of a falling tree, the silence of the forest returned. Jeff and Sam stood and looked around to see if everyone was safe. Luckily all had survived, but what they saw before them was complete and utter devastation. A swath of land approximately the width of two large men had been torn through the forest. As they gazed at the Wood, all they could see were fallen trees that edged the forest, and behind it, complete darkness.

"What was that?" Jeff asked Mas.

Mas glanced warily toward the Wood. "I think it was a 'Breathing.' I have only heard of them but have never seen one or the devastation that it brings. It is said that the old forest is so dense that nothing escapes through its canopies. The heat and the gases from the decaying wood build and build until finally they release, and since they can't go up, the wave takes the easiest path. Today we have seen the easiest path. Once it starts moving, nothing can stand in its way. Let's gather our things, for daylight will soon be upon us and surely this devastation will have woken many within the forest."

A few moments later, the sun started to crest the horizon in the East.

"It looks like a beautiful day to travel. Too bad we are not going toward the sunrise," Alina said.

They all looked up from their preparations, saw the gorgeous sunrise, and nodded their heads in agreement, knowing that north was the only direction they would travel until their task was completed.

"Hopefully the beauty of the day will carry us through to the other side," Yuma said as they all led their horses toward the opening of the Wood.

The beginning of the Wood was strewn with enormous branches, small twigs, and other debris from years of inactivity. It made travel with the horses difficult, as much of the wreckage had to be moved before they could pass. However, the further they moved away from the path of the Breathing, the less rubble littered the road. The group was now able to mount their horses, which helped them make better time traveling along the path.

As they moved further into the Wood, the light that funneled through the treetops was becoming fainter. Like most of the forest in this land, the trees were dying. The branches were so thick and entangled that when the leaves fell from the treetops, they became trapped and never reached the ground. They formed a blanket over the forest which prevented the sunlight from penetrating the Wood. It was like traveling during a moonlit night. But despite the lack of light and all the twists and turns, the road itself was easy enough to follow. The clip-clop of the horses' hooves on the rocks was a clear indication that they had not veered from the path.

As they rode, Jeff and Sam kept peering into the forest, trying to see what lay past the thick, entangled branches and trees. Once, they were able to see beyond a few feet into a small clearing. A murky pool of water glimmered with remnants of trees nudging their way out of the black depths.

"I can't imagine what could be living in that," Sam whispered to Jeff.

But Mas was close and overheard the conversation. "You

never want to go near a pool in this forest. Even though they are small, they are deep, and nobody knows what lurks there. You don't want to be the one who finds out."

They traveled quite a bit further when Jeff poked Sam and pointed into the forest. "Look, that's a pretty big clearing."

"The biggest one we've seen since entering the forest," Sam said.

The boys pushed their horses up to where Mas and the others were riding and pointed to the clearing.

Everyone dismounted and walked over to the edge of the road, gazing into the forest. Alina and Yuma looked at each other knowingly and walked deeper into the Wood. Mas, Jeff, and Sam followed them, leaving the horses on the road. After navigating their way through the brambles, they reached an opening. It was a path of broken trees and rubble that twisted and turned, and finally headed back, deep into the forest.

"This was made by the Breathing," Yuma said in a hushed voice. "These trees were just knocked down. The few leaves that are still clinging to the branches are wilting, but they were alive only a few short hours ago. Can you see the high area to the left where there is a stone outcropping and there is no damage? You can also see that everything below was destroyed. The Breathing followed the low valley. We had better get back to the trail."

They rode on and, a short while later, they came to a fortress.

"It's close to midday and we should give the horses a brief rest and get something to eat," Yuma whispered.

"I thought the fortresses would be bigger than this," Jeff said.

"As you can see, they are made from stone that had to be transported from the Northern mountains, which would have taken many men and much time," Yuma said.

"Why didn't they make them out of wood? There are so many trees all around here," Jeff said.

"These fortresses were meant to store provisions for the men crossing to the North," Mas said. "They needed to be strong to withstand the rigors of a damp forest. In these conditions, a wooden fortress would rot within a few years. However, the forest always takes what is hers and, by the looks of the fortress, she was starting to lay claim."

As they stood in front of the stronghold, the one door they could see had been bashed in and the few narrow windows had been shattered by invading vines. The top of the stronghold, once meant for men to keep watch for all who traveled this road, was overflowing with branches, leaves, and other remains left by the dense canopy.

After grabbing a bite to eat and a drink from their water bags, Jeff and Sam asked Mas if they could take a quick look inside the fortress.

"Be careful, and if anything doesn't feel right, leave immediately," Mas told them.

As they stepped inside, they could feel the cold dampness that had taken over the interior of the fortress. The room was large and littered with broken chairs, eating utensils, and tables. It must have served as the central room where meals and gatherings took place. Three doors were cut into the walls of the hall. The two doors on the left side were smaller and open. Both had a stream of dull light leaking into the main hall, which allowed the boys to barely see their surroundings. After taking a glance into the first room and finding nothing more than some old bunks, they moved on to the second room. All they found there were a number of empty shelves.

"They must have used this for storage," Jeff said.

As they left the storage room, they noticed a large double door at the end of the hall. This door was closed and only a piece of metal hung down where the door handle should have been.

"What do you think is in that room?" Sam asked.

"I don't know, but let's find out," Jeff said.

They saw that the heavy metal door latch had been torn from the door and thrown into the corner of the room.

"I wonder what did that?" Sam whispered.

"I don't think we'll ever know," Jeff said. "Hey, I'll bet it's where they kept all the weapons."

Sam nodded in agreement. When they were home, both boys loved playing with make-believe swords and creating pretend weapons. They were excited at the prospect of seeing more real ones.

A slight echo from their footsteps sounded as they walked across the stone floor. Just before reaching the back part of the hall, the boys stopped and looked at one another, each sniffing the air.

"What's that smell?" Sam said.

"I don't know, but it seems that the closer we get to this door, the worse it gets," Jeff said warily. "Maybe we should head back and tell the others."

"Let's get closer and see if we can hear anything," Sam said.

When they reached the door, they put their ears up against the thick wooden frame.

"Do you hear that?" Jeff whispered.

"Yeah, it almost sounds like someone snoring," Sam said.

"I think you're right. We should get out of here and tell Mas and Yuma," Jeff whispered.

As they left, Sam's cloak caught on the piece of metal that was once part of the door handle and, as he moved to leave, the door creaked and started to open. Sam stopped and released his cloak, but not before a thin stream of light had entered the room. With the door open, the smell that came from the darkness was so putrid that it burnt their eyes and made them gag.

"Oh, my goodness, what is that smell?" Jeff managed to say.

But before Sam could answer, they both realized that the snoring had stopped and another sound had taken its place—a low, guttural growl.

CHAPTER FOURTEEN
The First Encounter

"Let's get out of here!" Sam yelled.

The boys heard movement from inside the room and raced for the door. Just as they reached it, there came the sound of the door being smashed open. They stopped and turned to see what was there.

Jeff and Sam gasped at the sight of the creature that had burst through. It looked like a cross between a huge hyena and a grizzly bear. Its eyes were deep red with black at the centers, and drool dripped from its snarling mouth. A row of thorny spikes ran down its spine, extending to its the hind legs, which could be seen through its long and bristly black hair. The extended claws on its four feet scraped against the rock floor as it shifted nervously, waiting to pounce. The creature stared at the boys, its shoulders hunched above its lowered head.

"Stay still," Jeff said to Sam.

Suddenly, they heard something moving in the back room, something big.

"Run!" Jeff yelled, and they turned and bolted through the open door toward Mas and the others. The boys screamed for help, but before they could reach their group, something bounded over their heads and landed between them and their companions.

Alerted by the boys' warning, Mas and the others grabbed their weapons, which were never far from their reach, and ran to help. They were startled by a large beast that landed in front of them, but even more frightening was what was coming through the fortress doors. Muscles bulged from its short, hairy upper body. Its legs were long and boney, barely able to carry the massive weight of its body. It had the head of a wolf with red, calculating eyes, but these eyes indicated intelligence, unlike its companion. The creature's arms stretched down past its knees and from its hands protruded long, sharp claws. It raised a large club in a menacing threat to Mas and the others.

"What kind of creatures are these?" Mas yelled at Yuma.

"The large one is a Rogaru and it is the master of the hairy creature, which is known as a Dejan," Yuma said. "I thought this world was rid of them, but in this forest, one never knows."

The Rogaru stopped and let out a tremendous roar when he saw the men raise their weapons. The Dejan, which had been slowly stalking the boys, also stopped in its tracks. It seemed odd that both creatures appeared to be considering their next moves, but these two were unlike any foe that the group had ever encountered. Most creatures would just charge straight ahead, unthinking, with crazed anger in their eyes.

The Rogaru stood staring at Mas, his companions, and finally at the boys, who were separated from the group by the Dejan. He looked at everyone once, then one more time before emitting a few low, guttural sounds. As he did, the Dejan suddenly moved toward the boys and the Rogaru charged Mas and the others.

Even though the horses were nervous, they had been holding their place, but now they scattered. The confusion disoriented the Dejan and he started to follow some of the horses. Sam and Jeff were still cut off from joining their friends, but the chaos gave them just enough time for Sam to snatch up his backpack and for them both to grab their swords.

They ran into the Wood, hoping to circle around and join the others, but it was thick with branches and undergrowth, which slowed their progress. Then they heard crashing coming through the trees, and they both knew what it was. The boys decided they should run further into the Wood and possibly go around all the debris, but it was like an impenetrable wall and only led them deeper and deeper into the forest.

They kept running, but the sound following them was getting closer and closer. Because of their smaller size, Jeff and Sam were able to outpace their pursuer by squeezing through the dense trees. The Dejan was persistent, though, seeming not to feel the pain inflicted by ramming through the trees. The boys ran as fast as they could, crashing through branches, blocking their faces with their arms. Suddenly, they felt themselves slip down a long, muddy hill, sliding under bushes full of sharp thorns. When they reached the bottom, they grabbed a large branch, preventing them from falling into a deep crevice.

"Sam, are you okay?" Jeff asked, barely able to catch his breath.

"Just a little scratched up, but I'm okay," Sam said.

"Yeah, me too. Look at the size of those thorns! They must be an inch long. We're lucky they didn't tear us apart," Jeff said as he noticed his torn garments. A slight tinge of red was starting to ooze around the tears.

The boys knew they weren't out of danger yet, though, when they looked up and saw the menacing stare of the Dejan. Its teeth were bared and they could hear its low growl. Slowly and carefully, it started to make its way down the treacherous slope, trying to evade the sharp thorns. Suddenly it stopped, its path completely blocked by the thorn bushes. It was much too big to slide under them as the boys had done on their trip down the muddy slope.

The boys found their swords and stood to run when Jeff noticed something. He pointed to a very large patch of thorn bushes a few feet away from them.

"Quick, Sam, let's try to get in the middle of that bush," Jeff yelled. "Even that thing doesn't want to tangle with those thorns."

The boys ran to the thorn patch and crawled underneath a small open area, which was too small for the creature to enter without being torn apart by the thorns. However, the boys weren't taking any chances and used their swords to cut some of the branches to block the entrance. As they scooted further and further toward the center of the briar patch, they felt more than one or two thorns penetrate their clothing. Finally, they could go no further, and they hoped and prayed that this would be enough to deter the Dejan's wrath.

The creature took a mighty leap and landed where the boys had been standing a moment ago. It slowly walked around the large patch, looking for a way in. Finally, not seeing any easy entry, it started digging. Its claws were like shovels and it made quick progress as it dug deep, pulling the bushes out by their roots and avoiding the thorns. With every scrape of the Dejan's huge claws, it moved closer to the boys.

"Jeff, I don't think the thorns can stop it," Sam said.

"I have my sword and you know how sharp it is," Jeff said, trying to reassure his brother. "I'll be able to jab at the beast and maybe it will go away."

But it seemed that nothing would deter this animal from getting to its prey. Foot by foot, it advanced toward their location. The beast stopped and stared at the boys, knowing it was close to claiming its prize. It let out a guttural growl and then began its final dig.

"Jeff, stab it!" Sam yelled.

Jeff stuck his sword through the thorn bushes, trying to slash at the Dejan, but instead, he accidentally hacked off some of the bushes that had kept the creature at bay, allowing the Dejan to get even closer. The Dejan snarled at Jeff, trying to bite his sword.

With the thorns at their backs, the boys had nowhere to go as the creature advanced into the opening of their protective space. It lunged at them, avoiding Jeff's sword thrust. It pounced again, this time extending its huge claws. One claw caught Jeff's foot and ripped his boot. As pain coursed through Jeff's foot, he swung his sword and struck the Dejan above its shoulder. The animal cried out, briefly falling to the ground, its long tongue lapping at its wound like it was on fire.

Jeff got to his knees, swinging his sword at the beast in sheer rage. "You will not get us!" he yelled.

The Dejan, still feeling the sting of the blade, backed away as Jeff advanced like a crazed madman. The blade had done damage. The Dejan no longer had the advantage, for it could feel that Jeff's fear had vanished. Still, it stood its ground, snarling and hissing at the boys.

Jeff and Sam stayed within the safety of the thorn bush, Jeff still brandishing his sword. Then, from high above, they heard a deep and hideous call. The Dejan turned and left the boys, taking a long leap to the top of the slope to answer the summons of its master.

Jeff kept his sword pointed at the opening until Sam hugged him from behind.

"Jeff, that was great! I can't believe the way you protected us!" Sam exclaimed. "I'm so glad you chose the sword as a present from Azar. We would have been toast without it."

"I think you're right," Jeff said, his voice shaking.

"We should stay here for a little while to make sure the Dejan doesn't return," Sam said. "Hey, your foot is bleeding!"

Jeff looked down and realized that part of his boot was turning red. He took it off, and it was clear that the Dejan had grazed his foot with its claw.

"How bad is it?" Sam asked.

"It's not very deep or bleeding very much, so it should be okay," Jeff said. "Do you have any cloth that I could wrap around it?"

Sam pulled a small cloth from his pack and Jeff wrapped it around his foot.

"Are you okay?" Sam asked.

"It hurts a little, but I should be fine," Jeff answered as he put his boot back on.

They stayed in the safe space for a few more minutes, listening for any sound that would betray that the creature was still close.

"We should get back to Mas and the others now," Jeff said. "They may need our help."

They tried climbing to the top of the crevice through the same muddy trail that had brought them there, but it was too steep. They kept slipping down to the bottom of the hill.

"We need claws like that animal," Sam said.

Jeff nodded. "It would definitely help."

They realized that going up was not an option, at least not yet, so they walked along the narrow ridge until they could find a spot where they could climb up and join the others. Before long, they reached a rocky outcropping that allowed them to scramble up the slope. The rocks were slippery, and it was a treacherous climb. Halfway up, they came to a flat area. It was void of the brambles and brush they had been trampling through. It wasn't a large space, but it seemed out of place with the rest of the forest. Everywhere they looked, the small patch of land was covered in the brightest green grass and big clusters of colorful flowers with the most interesting shapes the boys had ever seen. Toward the back, where the land continued its upward climb, they saw dozens of small flowery bushes that had an incredible fragrance.

"That smell is amazing," Sam said as they walked over to enjoy the scent. But as they bent close to the shrubs to inhale the bouquet, they realized there was something behind them. "It looks like an opening," Sam said.

Jeff peered around the bush and saw an entrance to a small cave. "Should we go in?"

Sam nodded. "Why not?"

The boys squeezed around the bush and entered. The cave was dark, but the light from the outside filtered through the bush and gave them a dulled view of the cave. At first, they didn't think the cave was very deep, but once their eyes adjusted to the darkness, they were able to see more clearly. To the right, it looked as if someone had carved a small staircase into the rocks that led to a flat area about five feet above the ground. Beyond the flat spot, the boys could see what looked like another opening in the rock wall, and out of it shone a muted light.

"What do you think that is?" Sam asked.

"Let's get closer and find out," Jeff said.

They climbed up a few of the rocks and peered inside the opening. What they saw amazed them.

It looked like someone, or something, was living there. A fire smoldered in a tiny cooking pit where stones had been placed to funnel the smoke into a narrow hole above. Off to the far side of the hollow, a continuous flow of clear water trickled through the rocks and into a rock bowl. The overflow found its way out of the cave through a hole below the basin. The dirt floor was covered with several mats woven out of dried grass. A small bed sat in the corner, placed purposefully near the fire pit. Off to the side, clothing and cooking utensils filled several shelves that had been gouged out of the rock. Above them hung what appeared to be bags of dried herbs. Lastly, there was a little table and a cozy-looking chair. All in all, it looked like a very comfortable, secure, and homey set-up. The strangest thing about all of this, at least to Sam and Jeff, was the size of everything.

"What do you think lives here?" Sam asked.

"Not quite sure, but whatever it is, it sure is tiny," Jeff said. "We had better get going. We need to find Mas and the others."

As they left the cave and started to climb the remaining thirty feet to the top of the hill, they realized that the thorns that had saved them from the creature now prevented them from joining their companions, for they lined the top of the ridge for as far as they could see. There was no getting by them.

"We have to go back down and see if there is another way to the top," Jeff said.

On their way down the slope, Sam noticed something they'd missed when they first approached the cave. A small footpath, mostly covered in leaves, was visible from this height. When they reached the bottom of the slope, they could see how they had originally missed it. From where they stood, a large tree was partially blocking their view, but once they passed the tree, they had a full view of a winding trail that passed through a rocky outcropping and down into the valley below.

"In order to rejoin the others, we still must go up," Jeff said. "Unfortunately, I don't see any way to do that, do you?"

"Not unless we learn how to fly," Sam replied.

"Well, I guess we have to go down before we can go up," Jeff said.

With that, the boys took their first steps down the path, which clung to the side of the hill. Occasionally, an opening allowed them to view the valley below, but there wasn't much to see except for the treetops, which looked like a field of dead brush.

The further they walked, the narrower the path became, until finally they reached what appeared to be a dead end. A huge rock face blocked them from going any further. It hung over the valley like a watchful sentinel. The boys could just see around the rock, and it looked like the path continued, but there was no clear way to get over, around, or through the rock face.

"Now what do we do?" Jeff asked.

"Wait a minute. Look at the rock," Sam said. "There's a big crack that goes all the way to the other side and some spots above it that we could grab onto as we cross. If we're careful, I bet we could make it."

"I think you're right, and we don't have a lot of choices," Jeff said. "I also think that whatever lives in that cave uses this path all the time. It probably protects them against any large creatures, especially any four-legged ones. Look, the other side of the path is as worn as this side. Let's give it a shot, but be careful."

Sam pulled some rope out of his bag, and they tied it around their waists. Then they swung it around a tree trunk and, one at a time, slowly negotiated the rock face by deliberately placing their feet and hands in the positions that allowed them to cross without consequences. Finally, they reached the other side. Both gave a sigh of relief and continued down the path. It was narrow, with the occasional view of the valley below.

They kept looking up the hill to see if there was a possible trail or route that would lead them to the top of the ravine, but the masses of thorn bushes were too thick for them to navigate.

The boys had almost reached the bottom of the trail when they saw in front of them a strip of land that had been completely decimated. There wasn't a tree, bush or anything resembling growth left standing. The path of devastation wound through the forest like a snake, no reason for its course, and continued for as far as they could see.

"What happened here?" Sam asked.

"Sam, do you remember what Mas said about the Breathing when we were camped outside of the forest? I'll bet this is where it started," Jeff said. "Hey, wait a minute. Do you remember, just before we reached the first outpost, we could see the Breathing's debris from the road? We should be close to that area. If we walk along the path, we should be able to see the road. Once we find the road, it will be easy enough to find the group. That is if they are still there. Or still alive."

"What was that sound?" Sam whispered.

"I heard it too," Jeff said, "but I can't figure out what direction it came from. It sounded like someone, or something, is in pain."

Both boys stopped and listened. At first, all they could hear was the wind rustling the dead leaves. Just when they decided that what they'd heard must have only been the wind, the sound came again.

"It's coming from down below," Jeff said. "From that mess of fallen trees."

It was a groaning sound, but higher in pitch than you would expect from a person in pain. Still, they knew they had to investigate the sound, no matter what. As they reached the chaos below, the sound grew louder.

"Over there," Jeff said, pointing to a pile of debris left by the Breathing.

The boys cautiously walked toward the sound. It seemed to be coming from a mound covered with fallen branches and uprooted tree trunks. The pile of debris was thick, which made it very difficult to see anything inside. Jeff and Sam circled the pile, hoping to see or hear something.

Suddenly, Sam stopped and tapped his forehead. "How could I forget?" he said, reaching into his backpack and pulling out the ferret. "Maybe Cerith can help."

The ferret had been in a state of deep sleep in the darkness of Sam's backpack, but now she opened her eyes and became very animated. Cerith stopped and seemed to listen. She too heard the cry of pain. She jumped out of Sam's hand and ran directly toward the huge pile and disappeared inside it. After a minute, she poked her head out and seemed to summon the boys to her location.

They ran to the area and listened. Sam pointed. "It's coming from here!"

They began pulling and tossing the branches away from the pile, but then they came to a much larger limb that was preventing them from removing any more debris.

"Let me see if I can spot anything," Jeff said. As soon as he stepped onto the big branch that was holding everything in place, they heard a much louder cry from below. Jeff jumped off the branch and both boys peered into the pile. What they saw made them gasp.

CHAPTER FIFTEEN
Pejew

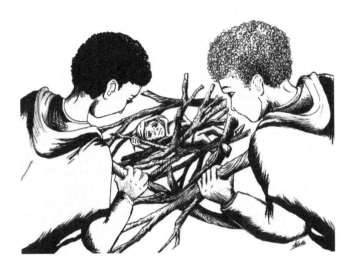

A little man no taller than six inches was pinned to the ground by the large tree limb. He was clearly fading in and out of consciousness, but when he saw the boys, a look of panic crossed his face. As he tried to escape, he let out a groan and grabbed his leg.

Knowing that he was stuck, the small being left his fate to the two boys, strange though they were.

"We have to get him out of there!" Jeff said to Sam.

Both boys grabbed their swords and began hacking

at the branch until they managed to cut through. They moved it just enough to reach the little man and lift off the branch. Now they could see that his leg was at an odd angle and was probably broken.

"Should we try to set his leg?" Jeff asked. "I learned about that in the Boy Scouts, but I'm not sure I can do it."

"Why don't we wait until we get back to camp?" Sam suggested. "Alina and Yuma may know what to do. I can put him in my pack. It's mostly empty and I have some soft cloth that we can pack around him to keep him stable."

"Good idea," Jeff said.

As Sam started to pick up the little fellow, his eyes opened. The boys could see that he was in pain, but he remained conscious.

"Are you able to speak?" Jeff asked in a kind voice. The little man nodded. "We have friends that are near the first outpost, and we hope they're safe. We were attacked by two animals, and we got separated. If we can get back to them, they may be able to help you."

"You must come with us. We will let you go once we finish helping you," Sam said. "My name is Sam, and this is my brother, Jeff. What is your name?"

"My name is Pejew, and I am a Peekado," the little man said weakly. "I live in the forest just above the ridge."

"I think we saw where you live, but what is a Peekado?" Sam asked.

"We are an ancient race of people who have traveled within different worlds for thousands of years. We seek knowledge, and when we find information that will help another civilization prosper, we pass it on to them. There are many who think we are ghosts, but we are not, that I can assure you."

"Why would they think that you're ghosts?" Sam asked.

"Have you ever thought you saw something out of the corner of your eye, but when you looked again, there was nothing there?" Pejew said. "If this has happened to you, you may have seen one of us."

"That's happened to me many times," Jeff said.

"Me too," Sam agreed.

"Well, during one of my travels, I got stuck here in Alfham, and I have never been able to return to my world or my family," Pejew said. "I have been alone for as long as I can remember."

"That is so sad," the boys said in unison.

Pejew shrugged. "We take life as it comes, and we make what we can out of it."

"How did you end up under all that brush, Pejew?" Jeff asked.

"I was foraging for food in the forest when I heard a terrible rumble, and before I could move, I was hit and buried by those branches and all the other debris. It pinned me to the ground, and if you had not found me, that is where I would have stayed."

"I'm so glad we found you," Sam said.

"So am I, and I thank you for your kindness," Pejew said. "May I ask what you are doing here? I don't see many men passing through this world. These are perilous times. Many dangerous creatures wander this forest."

"How do you know that we are men?" Jeff asked.

"My travels have taken me to many worlds. Yours is but one. But still, what are you doing in the world of Alfham?" Pejew asked again.

"We're traveling to the North country with a small group on a mission to save Princess Iris. There is a cone that will save her life and it lies within the mountains to the North."

"There lies a great danger," Pejew said. "The Dragon Attor inhabits the mountains in the North."

"We've heard about the dragon, but we've never heard its name before," Sam said.

"It is a creature that is pure evil. You must not go, for all who go perish," Pejew warned.

"We have to go," Jeff said. "We have to save the Princess or the world of Alfham will die. We also have to get back to our friends. They are in great danger. Do you know the quickest route to get back to the fortress that runs along the pathway?"

"Of course I do, it is that way," Pejew said, pointing down the trail into the forest.

Jeff carefully lifted Pejew and nestled him snugly within his pack, with only his head sticking out so he could guide them. They quickly reached the border of the forest where the Breathing had approached the road. As they scrambled through the forest to the road's edge, they could make out people yelling.

The boys ran in the direction of the calls. They came upon their horses and saw they were caught within the thick bushes, their bridles snagged by the thorns. They worked together to free their horses, then mounted them and rode as fast as they could to the fortress.

The closer the boys got, the louder the shrieks and shouts became. Just before reaching the fortress, they dismounted. Through the Wood, they could see the bedlam happening in and around the fortress. They grabbed their bows and arrows and ran toward the madness. Pejew huddled down in Jeff's bag for safety.

Yuma, Alina, and Mas had been battling the Rogaru and the Dejan for a long time and they looked exhausted. While Yuma and Alina fought the Rogaru, all of Mas's efforts were directed at keeping the Dejan at bay.

With Mas focused on the Dejan, the Rogaru now had an advantage over Yuma and Alina. He kept pushing them back and back. Only their skill as fighters kept them from being overpowered by the beast.

The boys could see that several arrows hung from the Rogaru's body like tiny needles clinging to a pin cushion. Yuma and Alina must have been able to release a few arrows before he'd charged, but his upper body was so muscular that the weapons couldn't penetrate enough to inflict a mortal wound. Even with all the arrows stuck in him, the Rogaru pressed the attack.

Yuma and Alina were fast and agile and able to avoid the awkward, wild swings of the Rogaru's club, but the battle had been raging for a long time and everyone was getting tired. Then it happened. Alina moved just in time as the club slid by her head, but Yuma slipped and fell to the ground while dodging the club, hitting his head on a rock. The Rogaru didn't waste any time and went to finish Yuma. He stood over him with a menacing glare, his club held high, and prepared for the final blow.

Alina was running to help Yuma when two arrows flew by her and found a spot under the upraised arms of the Rogaru. They were perfect shots. The club fell from his hand as he screamed in pain, for the arrows had found the only place on the Rogaru that wasn't full of thick, impenetrable muscle. The arrows penetrated deep within his underarm and continued on a path to his heart. The Rogaru stood over Yuma, swaying and unbalanced. Finally, he turned toward Alina, took two steps, and fell to the ground, never to take another breath.

Hearing his master's screams, the Dejan ran to the Rogaru's aid, but he never reached him, for two more arrows were launched into his hindquarters and, with that, the animal scrambled deep into the forest, leaving his master for good.

Everyone raced to Yuma to see how badly he had been injured. He tried to pull himself up, but Alina made him sit back down.

"Sit, we are safe. The Rogaru has been killed and his creature has run off into the forest. I don't believe we will see him again," Alina said.

Yuma looked confused. "What happened? I don't remember anything except for falling and hitting my head."

Mas stepped forward with an exceptionally proud look on his face as he turned to Jeff and Sam, who were still holding their bows.

"These two young boys came to our aid in the nick of time," Mas said.

Yuma thanked the boys for what they had done.

Jeff and Sam were happy to hear the praise from all their companions, but both felt a sadness in their hearts. As they looked at the Rogaru lying there, they knew they'd had no choice but to kill him. Yet somehow, it still made them feel miserable and tears filled their eyes.

Mas could see that the death of the Rogaru was bothering the boys. "Jeff and Sam, you did what had to be done. This creature would not have stopped until all of us were dead. It is his nature. You saved the life of Yuma, Alina, and possibly all of us. Death is never easy, especially if you are the one causing it. You need to understand that you had no choice."

The boys nodded their heads. They appreciated Mas's words and knew they were true.

"Should we bury him?" Sam asked.

"Unfortunately, we can't," Yuma said. "We must be on our way and the forest will take care of him. It is late and we still have a long journey ahead of us."

CHAPTER SIXTEEN
The Bow

The group went back and started to pack their belongings while Jeff and Sam walked down the road to fetch their horses. When they all gathered, the boys revealed to the others what had happened to them after the fight started. They told how the Dejan had chased them through the woods, how the thorn bush had saved them, how they'd found a hidden cave and what was inside that cave, but most of all, what Jeff had in the bag that hung from his shoulder.

As Jeff reached into his backpack, everyone looked at

him, and then back to Sam, wondering what was in the bag. Then Jeff pulled out Pejew.

The sight brought gasps from everyone.

"That's a Peekado!" Mas exclaimed.

"That's correct. How did you know?" Sam asked.

"I must admit that I wasn't exactly sure," Mas said. "I have only heard of them, but I thought their kind had passed from our world ages ago. There are still many stories told about their kindness and good deeds."

"His name is Pejew, and he says he will help us," Jeff said.

Alina was the first to notice that Pejew was in pain. "You're injured," she said to him.

"Yes, it happened during the Breathing," Pejew said weakly.

"Bring him here so that I may help him," Alina said. Like many in her settlement, she had been taught about curing ailments, fixing broken bones, and many other ways to cure people of their sicknesses.

Once Pejew was properly cared for and prepared for travel, they all mounted their horses and departed, leaving the Rogaru and the bad memories of this place behind them.

The rest of the day's travel was uneventful. The only sounds they heard were the scampering of a few small creatures running through the forest and the rustling of long-dead leaves that littered the floor of the woods. They still passed the occasional dark pool with gray skeletons of trees poking their heads out of the water. The trees seemed to grasp for the sight of the sun to bring them back to life, but the dark forest would not hear of it, so they continued their slow decay, becoming part of the pools that had taken their lives.

The group kept checking on Pejew. He seemed to be doing well as they traveled in silent companionship, keeping their thoughts to themselves.

Everyone could tell that night was starting to fall. What minimal light penetrated the forest canopy was starting to vanish, and what little heat the forest held was leaving, and with that, the sounds of the night began to spread through the forest.

"Jeff, do you smell that?" Sam asked.

"Yes, I do. It's a strange smell, but something is familiar about it," Jeff replied.

"I think it smells like rain," Sam said as they plodded along the trail and fell back into their silence.

They traveled for a while longer until Yuma finally broke the drudgery of the ride.

"I think that we are about midway, and there should be another fortress coming up soon," he said. "Hopefully, it will not be inhabited, for I fear that this night will bring a storm upon us."

A moment later, the boys felt the first raindrops fall on their faces from the canopy above. Far off in the distance, they could hear the rumbling of something much more ominous.

"Do you hear that? I think it's headed this way," Mas said.

Soon they came to the second fortress. It was like the first one in design, but larger and in better shape. The doors were still intact and supported with heavy hinges. The few windows on the side of the building still had most of their thick metal bars in place.

The last of the day's light was blocked from entering the forest by the storm clouds hastening the arrival of darkness.

Mas and Yuma were the first to dismount their horses, but not before Mas grabbed one of his blue stones for light.

"We'll go in and make sure there isn't anything or anyone inside," Mas told the others. "Have our horses ready for a hasty departure, for if something is lurking within these walls, we will want to leave quickly."

Alina pointed upward to the swaying forest canopy. "You may want to hurry. The wind is picking up and it is bringing a mighty storm with it."

The first good sign was that the door to the fortress was closed. They lifted the latch and pushed it open, and then cautiously entered the building. With the light from the stone, Mas and Yuma were able to explore the interior of the fortress. The building was like the first stronghold they had encountered: a bunk room with debris strewn on the floor, a storage room with broken shelves, and a room along the back wall with a closed door. But unlike the first fortress, the great room was enormous. It looked like it could seat fifty or sixty men for a large banquet. There were numerous broken benches and tables scattered on the floor. There was a large fireplace with a small stack of rotted firewood piled next to it. But mostly, the room was dry and secure.

Mas told Yuma, "If this storm gets bad, we may be able to have a fire and a warm meal. The wind and rain will disperse the smoke and confuse any who want to follow its trail."

Yuma nodded in agreement.

When they crossed the hall to the back room and slowly opened the door, they heard nothing but a few scampering mice. They could tell that this room must have been the storeroom because it was full of boxes and items hanging from the walls. They'd only begun exploring the room when Alina called out to them from the great room.

Yuma left to see what she needed, while Mas continued his search.

Yuma saw that Alina was soaked.

"Is it safe to come in?" Alina asked. "The storm is coming in strong, and the animals are getting restless."

Mas strode out of the back room and announced that everyone was clear to enter the building. Once they all came into the building and settled the animals, the storm really intensified. Even through the thickest forest canopy, they could feel the trembling of the thunder and see the brightness from the penetrating lightning.

"I guess we found this place just in time," Yuma said. "I think it is safe for us to have a warm meal tonight." The others nodded in agreement, so he walked over to the fireplace and started a fire.

"We were even luckier that nothing was living in the building," Sam said.

They all looked at him and started laughing. "Well said," Yuma declared.

"What's in the back room?" Jeff asked Mas.

"It's a storeroom," Mas said. "I couldn't fully investigate it, but it looked like a place to store weapons—what they call a weapons cache."

"A weapons cache!" both boys exclaimed.

"Can we go in and see what's there?" Jeff asked.

"Let me take another look before you go in," Mas said as he grabbed another of his blue stones and headed for the back door.

The boys waited patiently for Mas to return. They could hear his footsteps and were getting more excited by the second.

"Can we go in?" Sam asked.

After placing Pejew down near their companions and letting Cerith go in search of an evening meal, the boys removed their outer gear and their leather pouches, tossing them in a corner of the room. As soon as Mas said they could enter, they scooted by him with a blue stone that Eletha had given them.

Jeff and Sam discovered a very large weapons cache. The number of weapons was amazing, with all of them organized by group. There were huge swords meant to be wielded by large men during combat, smaller swords, long daggers with decorated handles, shields with colorful insignias, big crossbows, beautifully carved longbows, and every other type of weapon that the boys had ever seen during a medieval movie day.

They went up and down each of the aisles, holding and wielding each item. Finally, they reached the back of the room where the shields were kept. These weren't quite as exciting as all the other weapons, so the boys decided it was time to leave.

"Well, we'd better get back to everyone," Sam said. "I'm starving. I hope we can have something hot to eat. I'm getting tired of cold, dried food."

"Hey, what's this?" Jeff said to Sam as he turned to leave.

At the farthest corner of the room stood a stone box. It could have been missed as it blended into the outside wall and could easily have been mistaken for a small workbench. Now that the boys were close to it, they could see that it was a locked chest.

"What do you think is inside?" Sam asked.

"I don't know, but let's find out!" Jeff said. He grabbed a stone mace from the nearby rack and hit the lock once, then twice, but nothing happened. "This is a pretty strong lock."

Suddenly, Sam said, "Wait a minute," and dug into the small pouch that hung around his waist. He pulled out the key that had allowed them to enter the Garishes' stronghold. He slipped the key inside the chest's lock. It was a perfect fit. Click, and the lock opened.

Inside was the most magnificently carved bow the boys had ever seen. It had a beautiful recurve at each end, which was supposed to make the bow more powerful. The grain of the wood was tight, making it more flexible and adding distance and penetrating power to the arrow. It was packed in lamb's wool and next to it were three coils of sinew, used as bowstring and wrapped in animal fat to keep the string flexible. With the little experience the boys had, they still had never seen bowstring made like this. The material was black and almost felt like wire, but they knew by the feel that it wasn't metal.

"This must be a very special bow," Jeff said as he lifted it from the box. He grabbed one of the bowstrings and connected it to one end of the bow notch, but he couldn't make the connection to the other side.

"We should show this to everyone," Jeff said, and they

left the storeroom and entered the great room. "Mas, look what we found in the back."

Alina, Yuma, and Mas all gasped at the sight of the bow.

"I have never seen such a beautiful bow in all my life," Mas said, and the others agreed.

Jeff handed the bow to Mas and told him where they found it.

"I tried to string the bow, but I couldn't bend it enough to connect the string to the notch," Jeff said.

Mas tried to bend the bow to make the connection without success. Yuma and Alina both tried but had no more success than Mas and Jeff.

"There must be something we are missing," Alina said. She kept trying to connect the bowstring, but even she finally gave up.

"A bow is no good if you can't string it. You may as well put it back into its case," Mas said to the boys.

Sam picked up the bow to place it back in the box, and as he did, the bow began to vibrate, almost like a humming. He then felt a warmth passing from the bow into his body. No one else noticed. Suddenly, Sam felt himself removed from the room and transported to a different time. He was in the middle of a dark, burnt land and everything around him was burning. He held the bow in his hand and had a quiver of arrows strung to his back. One of the arrows notched into the bow had the darkest blade he had ever seen.

As Sam stared out into the devastated landscape, he wondered, *What would do this?*

Then he heard a screech and turned to see an enormous creature flying toward him. He froze in place, not able to pull his eyes off the dragon.

At that moment, he heard Jeff's voice. "Sam, come on, let's put the bow away."

Sam immediately snapped out of his trance, seemingly confused about where he was.

"Are you okay?" Jeff asked.

"Yes, but I just had a waking dream," Sam said.

The others looked at him, wondering what he meant.

Sam looked at them strangely, grabbed the bow, bent it, and easily strung it.

"How did you do that?" Alina asked, astonished.

Sam explained to the group what he'd experienced: the hum, the warmth of the bow, the burning land, the blacked-tipped arrow, but mostly, the dragon.

They all looked at Sam, and then at each other, trying to understand what this could mean.

"Sam, you mentioned a blacked-tipped arrow. Were there any of those with the bow?" Alina asked.

"We didn't see any," Jeff said, "but the chest was deep, and the bow was lying on top with lamb's wool surrounding it. Maybe the arrow was packed below the bow."

"Let's go back and check," Sam said, and they headed

for the storeroom, leaving the bow with the others.

The boys immediately ran over to the box and pulled out all the wool, looking for the arrows. To their disappointment, they didn't find any.

"That's strange," Jeff said. "Why would anyone pack a bow inside this heavy-duty chest and not leave any arrows with it?"

"It doesn't make a lot of sense," Sam said. "Let's look around to see if they may have put them elsewhere."

Jeff and Sam walked over to the area where the other bows and arrows were kept and searched everywhere, but they found nothing and returned to the chest.

"I would still like to keep the bow," Sam said. "After all, we have a quiver of arrows with us, and as much as I like the bow that Mas gave us, something is telling me that I should bring this one, too."

"I agree," Jeff said as he shut the lid of the chest.

"Did you hear that clunk when you shut the lid?" Sam asked.

"I sure did."

The boys opened the cover of the chest and looked inside, only to see the small remnants of wool that were used to pack and protect the bow. Just as they were about to close the lid again, Jeff noticed something small and circular that was partially covered by a little piece of wool at the bottom of the chest. It could easily have been mistaken for a variation in the stone, but on closer inspection, they realized that it was a button. They looked at each other questioningly. Sam reached into the chest and pushed the button.

The front of the chest's base slowly rose until it fully revealed its treasure. At the bottom of the chest, they saw a black quiver with streaks of silver and gold, filled with twenty arrows. Sam lifted the quiver and pulled out one of the arrows. As they had expected, the tips were as black as the deepest cave.

The boys quickly ran out to Mas and the others to show them what they'd discovered.

"Where did you find that?" Mas asked.

"There was a button on the bottom of the case and when we pushed it, a door opened and exposed the quiver of arrows," Jeff said excitedly.

Alina pulled one of the arrows out of the quiver and lightly touched the black tip. To her surprise, the tip of her finger started to bleed.

"Did you see that?" Yuma said.

Alina nodded. "I know. I barely touched it."

"What do you think the material is?" Yuma asked.

"I know what it is," Mas replied, and they all looked in his direction. "They call them dragon blades. They are dragon teeth fired in kilns deep within the bowels of our land. The heat is so intense that it hardens the teeth, turning them black. It is an ancient process long lost to even the most skilled blacksmiths. The blades are so sharp and strong that they can pierce stone itself."

"Can I keep it?" Sam asked the group.

"Well, since you are the only one who seems to be able to string the bow, I would say that it is calling to you," Yuma said, and everyone nodded in agreement.

Sam grabbed the bow and the quiver of arrows and laid them near the rest of his equipment.

After that, they filled their bellies with hot food. As they sat discussing tomorrow's journey, they noticed that the animals were uneasy. Jeff and Sam walked over and petted them to calm them down, but their nervousness persisted.

"We should all stay in one of the bunk rooms tonight," Yuma said. He opened the main door to try to discover the reason for the animals' edginess. Seeing only the lightning's flash and the deluge of rain, he was happy they had found this shelter. But just as he was shutting the door, it all stopped. Not another sound penetrated the building. The flashes of lightning that had dimly lit the area vanished, and darkness moved slowly toward the fortress.

Everyone gazed at Yuma, noticing that he had turned very quiet.

Yuma turned to them with a serious look on his face and said, "The Leshy comes."

CHAPTER SEVENTEEN
The Leshy

"Quickly, pull all the animals into the center of the room and gather as tightly as possible!" Yuma yelled.

Everyone moved swiftly to bring their belongings into the circle. The animals were restrained by tying their halters together, pulling them in as close as possible to the center. Remembering what Eletha had told them, they all reached inside their pockets and grabbed their blue stones. The light from the stones was immediate, illuminating the room in a bluish hue. They stared at the door, waiting.

"Is everyone here?" Alina asked.

Yuma looked around. "I can see everyone except for Cerith."

"There she is," Jeff said, pointing near the horses.

"What's going to happen?" Sam asked Mas.

"We must wait and see," Mas said. "This story is not over. There are many chapters that must be written and only we can write them. We have passed many trials on our way, this being only one of them. Have faith in yourself and your companions. I think you will find that this will get you through almost anything. Remember, never give up."

The door remained closed. The thrashing of the branches within the forest was silenced. The windswept rain stopped pounding against the walls of the fortress. The flashes of lightning no longer appeared through the barred windows. The darkness was coming. It was like a fog slithering through a cool river valley, silent and incessant in its pursuit to obscure all that exists. Soon, the walls were as dark as the deepest mines. The fire that had been blazing only a short time ago and giving warmth to the group grew cold and dead.

Their circle of light from the blue stones held like a fortress against the persistent assault of the darkness. Except for their circle, only the area that led into the weapons cache was still visible, and that light was slowly being extinguished. That's when Jeff noticed his pouch next to the door.

Jeff grabbed Sam and pointed to where their pouches and outerwear lay in the corner.

"What?" Sam asked.

"Those are our leather pouches!" Jeff exclaimed.

"I'm so glad that Pejew isn't still in mine," Sam said.

"Yeah, but guess what?" Jeff said. "That's where I have the Crystal of Paladin. I should run and get it."

As he said those words, the area by the weapons cache turned black and the sight of their belongings disappeared into a thick ooze of darkness. Without warning, the outer door was thrown from its hinges, one half landing in the group's ring of light and the other half into a ghostly black wall.

"Don't touch that door," Alina warned. "It may pull you into a place of darkness, and I am not yet sure what prowls within its shadows."

Nothing entered, or at least nothing they could see, but they all knew something was now within the hall because the animals were becoming more and more agitated.

"Mas, do you feel its presence?" Alina asked.

"I think we all can, especially the animals," Mas said. "And it is getting harder to keep them calm. Be thankful that these stones are still shining so bright."

"What should we do?" Yuma asked.

"We wait and see what the Leshy does," Mas replied.

Alina looked at Jeff, and something in her head clicked. "Jeff, do you have the Crystal of Paladin?"

Everyone turned to Jeff, waiting for his answer, and by the look on his face, they knew the answer was not good.

"I had it in my leather pouch for safekeeping, but when we came out of the storm into the weapons room, I took it off and put it in the corner," he said. "I'm so sorry. I meant to put it back on, but I got so excited about the weapons room that I forgot. I should have kept it with me and never taken it off."

"Jeff, these things happen, and we are still safe," Alina said. "However, if we are ever going to get out of here, we will need to figure out a way to retrieve that pouch."

The silence reminded the boys of when they'd entered the Garish caves, but this time they could see everyone, at least inside the circle. They kept looking into the darkness, hoping to get a glimpse of what might be on the other side.

"There, did you see that?" Sam shouted, pointing to a spot in the blackness.

"What did you see?" Mas asked.

"It was like a shadow moving inside the darkness," Sam said. "It disappeared as soon as I saw it. But I think it looked right at me."

"Do you recall what Eletha told us?" Alina asked. "The Leshy is part of the forest. It can show itself as a spirit. It can take on the form of forest animals, but mostly, it will show itself with human features. As Eletha said, it was once human but was cursed by black magic, and now it tries to return to what it once was."

"I believe it is trying to judge our strength," Yuma told the group. "I'm sure that it didn't expect to confront the barrier created by the blue stones."

It seemed like an eternity before anyone else spoke. The fear of the unknown kept everyone on edge. Each person was scanning the darkness, hoping to catch a glimpse of the slightest movement. Time and silence started to play tricks on them. They saw movement in front of them, behind them, and then above them. They heard scraping on the floor and then on the ceiling. Muted wails, yelps, and screams echoed from deep within the darkness.

"What are those noises?" Sam asked Mas.

"It's trying to agitate and frighten us," Mas said. "It wants us to bolt from the circle, but we must remain strong. If the sounds start to bother you, try to cover your ears."

The boys went over to cover the horses' ears with their sleeping blankets, but this seemed to do very little to comfort the animals. The shrieks and yelps continued to get louder and louder. Even the strongest person's nerves would become strained through this onslaught, never mind the animals, who did not understand anything that was happening. Time moved on, and so did the chaos.

The boys could hear Mas, Yuma, and Alina saying that their only chance of survival was to retrieve the Crystal of Paladin. But how? Each one of them suggested a plan.

"The size of our circle has changed," Alina said. "It's getting smaller."

"Look at the door," Yuma said, pointing. "At first, half the door was visible, and now it's almost completely engulfed by the darkness. Our blue stones must be weakening. Soon their power will be completely diminished."

"We have to retrieve the Crystal of Paladin," Mas said.

"Mas, I know where it is, and the Crystal has the connection with me," Jeff said. "I need to be the one who gets it."

"And I am going with him," Sam said, looking at his brother.

Jeff looked back at Sam and smiled.

"We can't let you go. It is too dangerous," Alina warned.

"Alina, I'm afraid that Jeff is right," Yuma said. "He has a connection to the Crystal and that may guide him to it."

"I don't like it, but I agree with Yuma," Mas said.

Pejew spoke up. "I will also go with them. I am of the forest, so maybe the Leshy will see that and let us pass."

"I'm going to take Cerith," Sam said. "She is also of the forest, and even though she may not be able to see, she has a great nose, and maybe she'll be able to smell Jeff's pouch."

"That's a great idea," Alina said.

An understanding of what must be done passed through the group without any further discussion.

Jeff grabbed another leather pouch and placed Pejew inside, then slung it over his shoulder. Sam put Cerith on his shoulder, a spot she had become comfortable with.

"I imagine we're not going to be able to see much once we leave the circle, so we should tie ourselves together with this rope," Jeff said. "That way, we can't get separated."

"Good idea," Mas said.

"Do you think we should take any weapons with us?" Sam asked.

"According to Eletha, the only thing that will protect us from the Leshy is light, so leave your weapons here," Alina said.

The boys quickly tied a loop of rope around their waists, said goodbye to their companions, and then walked into the darkness.

CHAPTER EIGHTEEN
Into the Darkness

I t was like walking into a dense, heavy fog. The air was thick, and it made breathing difficult. The one blue stone only created a very small circle of light, so the boys could barely see each other. Even though they were tied together by the rope, they decided to move closer and hold hands. As they did this, they bumped into each other and Cerith fell from Sam's shoulder and onto the ground.

They felt along the ground, trying to find her. They whispered her name, but she didn't come.

"Sam, don't call out her name. She will either find us or she will find her way back to the others," Jeff said.

Sam nodded his head in agreement, for they didn't want the Leshy to hear them and know they'd left the protection of the circle. If they were fast enough, they could find his pouch, grab the Crystal of Paladin, and save everyone.

The boys and Pejew walked in the direction of the pouches. After a few minutes, Jeff stopped and whispered to Sam, "I'm not sure why we aren't there yet. I wonder if we got turned around when we bumped into each other."

"Just go a little further," Pejew said.

After walking a little longer, Jeff stopped. They crouched down to see if they could glimpse the packs. They got close to the floor and cupped the stone to dull the light as much as possible. All they could see was the floor.

Suddenly, something whisked by Sam and touched his back. He jumped up but didn't yell out.

"Something just touched me and then it was gone," Sam whispered.

"I wonder if it knows we're here," Jeff said.

The air around them began to turn cold. Wisps of air passed by their faces. Then they heard a low voice in the mist of darkness.

"Jeff and Sam, where are you? It's Christmas morning

and we can't find you. Where did you go? Please come home."

The boys heard someone crying. The crying became a wailing, and then a screeching. "Come home, please come home, I miss you so much. Why did you leave me?"

"Jeff, that's Mom. She's calling for us."

"Remember what Eletha said about the Leshy," Jeff said. "It plays with your mind. It tries to distract and trick you. She said not to listen to the voices. Cover your ears. That isn't Mom. She doesn't know we're here."

"I know, but it sounds just like Mom," Sam said.

"You need to block it out of your head. We have to keep searching."

Almost as soon as Jeff had spoken, the wailing stopped.

"The voices are gone," Sam said.

"I know," Jeff whispered. "Let's keep searching. We need to find the Crystal and we should be there by now. Our gear was only a few steps from us, and we've been walking in a straight line for a while."

"You're right," Sam said. "Hey, do you smell that? It smells like an old fire."

They looked down and saw that they were standing next to the fireplace.

"In the darkness, we must have gotten turned around and walked the wrong way," Jeff said.

"Look, the light of my stone is becoming weaker. What

if we are lost in here forever?" Sam said worriedly.

"We'll be fine. We're still in the fortress, and we should be able to find my pack."

"What if the Leshy finds us first?" Sam asked.

"I think it knows we are here, but maybe it's occupied by Mas and the others. It probably sees them as more of a threat than us."

The boys walked in a different direction but only found more darkness. They were starting to get concerned.

"Jeff and Sam, put your hands in front of you," Pejew told them. "If you feel something that you recognize, it may help us figure out where we are."

They walked a few more steps.

"Wait, I feel a wall," Sam said.

"That's good. Now, walk in one direction and slide your hands along the wall," Pejew instructed. "Let's see where we end up. Maybe we'll reach the bunk room or the storeroom. From there, we should be able to find the pouch."

Jeff and Sam felt their way along the wall until Sam said, "I think I found one of the doorways. I can't feel the wall any longer."

"Don't stop touching the wall," Jeff said. "If this is the storeroom and we keep our hands on the wall until we find the other side of the door, our packs should be a few feet away. That may take longer, but at least we won't get lost again."

About halfway across the room, they stopped. The room had changed. Something had entered. A chill went up Sam's back. Then a raspy, menacing voice cut through the darkness.

"Did you think that you could escape me? Nothing enters without me knowing. This is my domain. I am the darkness."

The boys couldn't tell which direction the sound was coming from, so they simply froze and held each other. They turned and scanned the room for any possible movement of the Leshy.

"If we run for the door, we might be able to reach the circle of light, but now I'm not sure which way to go," Jeff whispered.

"We could run right into the Leshy," Sam said.

"You can't escape," the voice hissed. "Once you left the protection of the circle of light and entered my darkness, your fate was sealed. The power of the blue stones is fading and soon their protection will be gone."

"What is it that you want from us?" Jeff asked.

"You and your companions have come into my forest and killed one of my creatures. I am the guardian and protector of all creatures that dwell here."

"But he tried to harm us," Sam said. "We were only traveling through the forest and had no intention of harming anything. We were only protecting ourselves. All we want is to get to the other side of the forest."

"As soon as the power of the blue stones subside, you will suffer the same pain that your companions have suffered," the voice hissed.

"What do you mean?" Jeff yelled.

"See your companions and their animals," said the Leshy.

A tunnel of vision appeared in the darkness, showing the main hall. There lying in a circle were the bodies of Mas, Alina, Yuma, and the animals.

"What have you done to them?" Sam yelled.

Sam began to cry, while tears formed in Jeff's eyes. Hopelessness and despair filled them both.

"Sam, maybe they're okay. It might be that the Leshy is trying to frighten us again," Jeff said.

"Oh, I hope so," Sam said.

Then the boys heard something being dragged across the floor.

"Do you hear that?" Jeff asked.

"I do," Sam replied.

The sound stopped right at their feet. They remained still, not daring to move. Then Sam felt something pull at his pant leg. He bent down and felt Cerith and a leather pouch.

"That dragging sound was Cerith," Sam whispered. "I think she found your pouch!"

Jeff bent down and felt around the floor.

Pejew, who was still inside the bag on Jeff's shoulder, whispered for him to be careful.

Jeff recognized the feel of his pouch. It was right by his foot, so he carefully reached inside. He touched the roundness and the warmth of the Crystal of Paladin. As he did, the Crystal started to vibrate.

"I know what it is that you feel. It can't help you for this is my world," roared the Leshy.

The voice of the Leshy lost its sharpness and he lunged at Jeff, just as the full power of the Crystal exploded with a flash so bright that all within the room were blinded.

The Leshy cried out in pain and froze in place, locked in a vice stronger than any magic it could separate. The force of the Crystal had severed the rope that bound the boys together and thrown Sam against the back wall of the room. When his eyes finally adjusted to the light, he gasped at what he saw.

Jeff, Pejew, and the Leshy were locked together in a ball of light. None of them moved, staring at each other as if they were in a trance.

The Leshy had shown itself. The swirling shadow that Sam had seen earlier had all but disappeared. It had taken its human shape, but most of it was covered by a dark cloak. Blackness filled the void where its face should have been. But in that blackness, piercing green eyes with red centers stared straight at Jeff. A thin, bony hand clutched Jeff's shoulder, the claw-like nails digging into his flesh until spots of blood appeared.

Sam carefully approached the ball of light. He could feel the vibration radiating from the Crystal. He reached out and touched the ball, which was as hard as stone.

Sam raced around the globe of light, probing and testing it for any possible way to free Jeff and Pejew. He stumbled on a piece of wood on the floor and grabbed it. He beat the sphere of light, trying to release his brother from its prison. Finally, his arms gave out and he threw down the piece of wood and slumped onto the ground.

As he stared into the light, Sam remembered what Eletha had said: "But I warn you, only use the Crystal's power if all else fails. For if no solution is found, you may be locked into the circle of light searching for eternity."

CHAPTER NINETEEN
Into the Light

Where there had been complete darkness, there was now only light. Jeff could feel the Leshy's touch, but there was no pain. Pejew was in his mind, the Leshy was in his head—what was happening? His mind was whirling as if small explosions were going off in his brain. And then, calmness and clarity. Jeff, the Leshy, and Pejew were of one mind, probing and exploring each other's thoughts and memories.

Now it was like a dream, with Jeff and Pejew sitting above it all. A large village was spread out at the base of a huge mountain, and there were people everywhere. There were people buying food, others selling wares, older children caring for their siblings, and jokers entertaining all that would listen. It reminded Jeff of when the family would go to a farmer's market. Happy people living life.

Suddenly, the people stopped. The world beneath their feet was rumbling and shaking. They looked to the peak of the mountain as a large cloud of smoke and dust exploded into the sky. Then the rocking of the land stopped, but the steady stream of ash continued to fill the sky until day became twilight, obliterating the sun's light. Something was in the cloud. There in the sky, a creature was flying toward the village. It was the color of black ash. At first, the people didn't know what it was, but they knew it was something horrible. They were immobilized by fear. Then, fire rained down on the crowds, an inferno so intense that even in his dream-like trance, Jeff could feel the heat. Within minutes, everything had been turned to ash. Nothing survived, not even a blade of grass.

What could do something like this, killing so indiscriminately? Jeff wondered. Tears slowly fell across his face. *How could anything be so cruel and merciless?*

Jeff had never seen a creature so large. The biggest animal he'd ever seen was an elephant, and this creature was twice the size. Jeff wondered how it could keep itself in the air. It was as black as coal, with a wingspan wider than any plane. Its chest bulged with power. The four legs that emerged from its body had claws that would penetrate the thickest steel. It was an awesome sight to behold. Jeff had only seen these creatures in movies and books about mystical creatures. He knew what it was: a dragon. To comprehend that these creatures really existed muddled his mind. He watched the dragon's flight until it finally vanished somewhere high on top of the mountain.

Then he saw a lone man running from the forest toward the village. Something was familiar about this person, but at that moment, Jeff couldn't place him.

When the man reached the ash-ridden town, he found nothing but death and destruction. He slumped and released a river of tears for his family. Everything had been taken away from him in an instant. *If only I had been here to help*, the man thought. Grief and guilt tore at his heart.

The man stood and looked skyward, yelling into the air, "I am Elon, and one day I will avenge my family!"

Who was this person? Then it all came together. Even in the state Jeff was in, he understood what was happening. Somehow, Elon *was* the Leshy.

After days of grieving and with everything in his life gone, Elon turned and slowly entered the forest, not knowing that the woods would become his prison. He walked deep into the forest. In a bewildered state, he looked around, not knowing where he was. Finally, exhausted, he lay on the mossy ground and fell into a troubled sleep. When he woke, a very old man was standing over him.

"My name is Erid," the old man said. "What are you doing so far into the Wood?"

Elon told him his terrible story, and then the wizard walked him further into the forest. They finally reached a small clearing, bright and green. Next to a brook stood a little stone cottage. It was surrounded by many different types of animals. Elon's first thought was that these animals shouldn't dwell together, for they were natural enemies, but they seemed as comfortable with each other as he had been with his children.

"These animals are mortal enemies. How are they existing with each other?" Elon asked.

"Around my home, all the creatures are protected by me," Erid said. "Once they leave the protection of my dwelling, nature takes over and they do what comes to them by instinct. That is the way of the natural world, and that I will not change. Come into my home and I will tell you my story."

Elon went with him into the cottage. They sat down and Erid began his tale. "I am the keeper of the forest and have been for as long as I can remember. I have seen you walking through the woods many times, and I know that you love being here. I am old and soon my time in this world will be finished. I need someone to pass on my knowledge to, someone who will care for the creatures and the forest as much as I have. I know that you have lost everything dear to you—your home, your friends, but most of all, your family. Let the Wood become your new family and take care of it. Can you find it in your heart to take my place?"

Maybe it was despair and loneliness, or maybe it was a new sense of purpose that made Elon accept a new life. "Yes, I will," he told Erid.

Months passed and Elon learned much from the keeper of the forest. Unfortunately, the wizard's health continued to decline. The keeper showed Elon all the good magic that he could. One day, while Erid was out walking in the forest, Elon noticed a book that he had not seen before. When Erid came back from his walk, Elon questioned him about the book.

"This book contains the darkest of all magic," Erid said. "A curse on all mankind. If I could destroy the book, I would."

"Then why do you keep it?"

"I keep the book safe so this magic will never be used, for there are those who would engage in this magic for the wrong reasons," the wizard said. He grabbed the book and placed it high on a shelf. "Never touch this book again, for only pain will follow you," he warned Elon.

Another year passed and, with that, so did Erid. The forest kept Elon occupied, but with the wizard gone and no one to speak to, loneliness seeped into his heart. Thoughts of his lost family brought anger and pain. The idea of revenge slowly filled his every thought, and that is when he remembered the book. He reached up to the shelf and took it down.

Elon thought there must be a spell inside that would make him more powerful than the dragon. Then he could defeat it. He studied the book. He found what he was looking for, a spell that allowed him to conjure "Hell's Fire." *This could certainly destroy a dragon*, he thought.

Having heard what the wizard had said about the evil of the book, Jeff knew that nothing good could be had by examining it, so he screamed to Elon, "No, don't do it!" But he realized that his cries would fall on deaf ears, for he was seeing the past and that was something he could not change. Jeff watched as Elon took a deep breath and then cast the spell.

Immediately, darkness crept around the cottage and the surrounding woods. The animals felt the change and left the safety of the cottage.

Magic is like a prickly pear. If you manipulate it correctly, it can be a delicious treat, but one wrong slice and it can give you a mean cut. Unfortunately for Elon, he sliced it in the wrong direction. In casting the spell, his words had failed, as did the spell. His body shriveled and his mind turned black. He was still trapped by his promise to protect the forest, but he would live it in Hell. Like him, the beautiful forest turned dark and tangled. The Leshy was born.

While Jeff and Pejew were seeing how the Leshy had come to be, the Leshy was also seeing inside their minds.

The Leshy could see that Jeff had a loving family and a beautiful home. He was here to save a princess's life and rescue a world that was foreign to him, risking his own life to save others. The Leshy saw that he would have to travel through the mountains in the North, the land of the dragon. The same dragon that had taken everything from him.

This dragon took everything from me and now it could take everything from this young boy, the Leshy thought.

The Leshy turned to Pejew and saw that he had lost everything too, but his heart was still pure and good. Something inside the Leshy was softening. This display of loss and love was melting away the dark magic that had turned him into a black and malicious being.

Jeff felt it first, a lightness in the air. Jeff looked at Pejew and said, "I think the Crystal has found a way to destroy the darkness of the Leshy."

The show of love Jeff had for his family had brought back feelings the Leshy hadn't sensed for a long time. He felt himself changing. Everything was getting brighter, and then he saw his own family, only as a memory, but a clear remembrance of all that really mattered.

Jeff was also seeing everything clearly. The fog in his mind vanished. He could see that the three of them were still surrounded by a ball of translucent white. The contorted face of the Leshy was softening, and tears dripped down his twisted features. Each teardrop tore away at the prison that held them until, finally, the light from the Crystal faded, as did the darkness in the room.

The boys heard their companions shouting, "Jeff! Sam! Where are you?"

"We're in here!" Sam shouted back.

Within seconds, Mas, Yuma, and Alina rushed into the barracks chamber, weapons drawn and at the ready.

Sam ran toward them. "Oh my God, we thought the Leshy had killed you. I'm so happy you're okay!"

The sight of Jeff, Pejew, and a shriveled old man lying in a heap on the floor stopped them in their tracks.

"What is this?" Mas cried out.

"We found the Crystal of Paladin and then the Leshy found us," Sam explained. "When Jeff grabbed the Crystal, it burst and captured Jeff, Pejew, and the Leshy in a sphere of light. Then something happened and it disappeared."

Alina and Sam went over to Jeff and Pejew to help them stand up.

"Are you okay?" Alina asked them.

"Yes, we are, but what about him?" Jeff said, pointing to the Leshy. "His real name is Elon, and his story is very sad."

The Leshy lay on the ground, his appearance totally changed. His true face—Elon's face—was now revealed. It was older, but all the pain had been wiped away. Unfortunately, his body was old and the power of the dark magic that had kept him alive was now leaving him. Life was fading from his body.

Elon motioned to Jeff and Pejew to come close. "I am dying," he whispered weakly. "I have knowledge that would be valuable to your quest. I have seen where you need to go. I have traveled to this place in my past life. At the base of the mountain, near a stone resembling a sword, you will find a passage that will take you to the destination that you seek. Beware, for there are other beasts that live in those tunnels."

Elon looked up at Pejew. "I have been the master of this forest and I let my want for vengeance rule me, a regrettable failure. The Wood has become darkened under my watch, and so have its creatures. The forest was beautiful long ago, and with you as its guardian, it can be that way again. Let the land be your family and do with it what I couldn't."

"I have lived in this forest for so many years," Pejew said. "It is now my home and there is nothing that would please me more than to become its caretaker."

"Go now, finish your mission," Elon told Jeff. "The Wood will no longer impede your progress." And with that, Elon, the man who had been the Leshy, closed his eyes, took his last breath, and faded into dust.

CHAPTER TWENTY
Finding the Entrance

The group gathered all their belongings, packed the horses, and prepared to leave.

"I will travel with you to the edge of the forest," Pejew told them.

After a half day of travel, they reached the edge of the Wood. When they first peered out of the forest, they all stared, trying to comprehend the vision that lay before them: a massive mountain reaching into the sky, and a wasteland filled with burnt trees, stumps, and stones scorched by fire.

Tears ran down Alina's face as she realized the damage that had been done to their world. "This creature is pure evil, so we must be very careful when entering its realm. Before leaving the cover of the forest and becoming visible to the dragon, we should view the surrounding land. It may allow us to get a glimpse of the landmark that the Leshy told us about."

"I agree," Mas said. "I don't believe anything that stays visible would survive here. We are lucky that the forest grows so close to the mountain. Let us hope that the entrance under the mountain is nearby."

They all searched for glimpses of anything that resembled a stone sword, but they saw nothing.

"A few of us may have to take a chance and leave the safety of the forest to see if we can find the landmark," Yuma said.

Suddenly, Mas stopped and looked to the sky. He reached into a small pouch that was tied to his belt, pulled out his whistle, and blew.

A moment later, Windsong the eagle screeched from high in the sky and raced toward the forest. He landed on Mas's outstretched arm. Alina and Yuma were at first surprised, then smiled at Mas. Mas spoke to the eagle in a language strange to them, and then Windsong was soaring high above the mountain, searching for the entrance. Soon he drifted lower in the sky and seemed to be circling a particular spot.

Mas pointed to a very rocky area of the mountain. "He's found it. There, behind that outcrop of boulders, is the entrance."

"Are you sure?" Yuma asked.

"The eagle's eyes are sharper than any of ours," Mas said. "He knows what we look for and, as you can see, he has not left that area. We either expose ourselves to the creature that lives within by searching the mountainside, or we trust what Windsong is seeing. He has already proven himself once during our venture. I'm sure that he's circling the entrance."

"Then let us prepare to leave," Yuma said. "It isn't far, but we must stay hidden until we reach the entrance. We will leave the horses behind and carry only what we need."

The group grabbed their weapons and what little food they had left. In their hands, the weapons seemed insignificant to the task they were about to undertake, but if they were lucky, they would never have to use them to battle the dragon. Their task had nothing to do with destroying it and all to do with bringing back the cones from the forest that lay beyond the mountain. If they could only get to the other side without being discovered, they might never encounter the monster that lay within.

Pejew looked up at Jeff and Sam. "I owe you my life, and because you made me part of your group, I now have a purpose. I will make this forest as beautiful as it once was. The horses will follow me, and I will protect them until you return. The forest will welcome you back for a safe journey home."

Pejew bid them farewell and walked off into the forest.

Mas, Yuma, Alina, and the boys all looked toward the area Windsong was still circling.

"There, that looks to be the best and quickest way to the rock outcropping," Mas said.

They still couldn't see the stone resembling the sword that marked the passageway under the mountain, but in their hearts, they were hoping that it was there.

Alina pointed. "See there, toward that large stone. That seems to be a flat area. Maybe it was once a path that led to the entrance."

"Alina, you're seeing something that I can't. You should take the lead and we will all follow you," Mas said.

"If we run, we should be able to get there quickly," Alina said.

Jeff and Sam seemed anxious to make the crossing. They had both run for long periods of time up and down the beach and through the woods back home, but they had never faced the consequences that this short run held. All they had to do was make it to the spot that Windsong was showing them and enter the passageway. If they could do that without being seen by probing eyes, they could all breathe easier.

Alina was strong and a very fast runner. Thankfully, her companions were able to keep up with her pace. They leapt over fallen trees, jumped over small rocks, and when necessary, climbed over boulders that blocked their path. They were within a stone's throw when they saw the boulder that was shaped like a sword. It had been toppled by a force that had split it in two. It had burn marks on it, and that only meant one thing—the dragon had destroyed it. When they finally reached the site, they realized that it wasn't the only thing that had been damaged.

The cave entrance had been destroyed by a landslide of boulders and smaller rocks.

"Now what are we going to do?" Sam asked Mas worriedly.

"First of all, let us take cover," Mas told everyone. "We don't want to be caught in the open."

As they all hid behind a large boulder, Jeff thought he saw an opening high above and decided to climb the rocks to see what was there.

A minute later, Yuma asked, "Where is Jeff?"

"There he is," Sam said, pointing high into the rock pile.

Mas quickly left the cover of the boulder and called Jeff to come back down, but Jeff kept climbing. When he finally stopped, he motioned for Mas and the others to follow him.

"I think I've found a small opening into the tunnel," Jeff shouted. "It's blocked by large stones, but I think they can be moved."

When his companions climbed up and reached him, they saw that he had found an opening.

"I'm not sure how far down it goes," Jeff said, "but you can feel a strong draft of air coming out of the hole."

Mas grabbed his glow stone and put his hand into the hole to try to see how deep it was. "I can't see very far, but it looks like there are rocks that we can climb down and maybe get to the bottom. We just need to move these two stones so that we can enter the tunnel."

Yuma and Mas were able to move the first stone without too much trouble. The second, much larger stone seemed to be wedged on both sides of the opening. If they could only move one side, the boulder would fall through and land on the floor of the cave—however, it wasn't budging.

Mas grabbed his sword, hoping that it would help him move the stone. He hit a smaller rock, which rolled down the hill, hitting another rock and then careening into a larger stone, creating a minor landslide. By the time it was finally over, anything that had ears would have heard the clatter. Everyone froze and scanned the skies. All they could see was the eagle flying ever higher.

Suddenly, Windsong let out a piercing screech. Mas knew what that meant.

"Quickly, let's see if we can move the stone," Mas called to everyone. Suddenly, they felt the ground tremble and heard a dull roar coming from somewhere within the mountain.

Mas and Yuma tried chipping away at one edge of the rock with their swords to see if they could move it, but their swords only clanged against the hardness of the stone.

Then Jeff remembered the time back in the valley of the Garish when his sword had pierced stone.

"Wait a minute, let me try!" Jeff yelled.

He grabbed his sword, raised it high above his head, and took a mighty swing. Unlike the noise the other swords had made, Jeff's sword sliced easily through the stone with a swooshing sound. When the two halves fell to the bottom of the cave, the entrance was clear.

Everyone was amazed at what Jeff had accomplished with his sword.

"Quickly! We must hurry and get inside," Mas said. One by one, they climbed down the wall of stones to enter the tunnel.

Mas was the last person to climb down. Before descending into the darkness, his final vision was of something massive taking flight from the top of the mountain and heading toward them. He knew what it was, and it chilled his heart, but there was nothing he could do other than slide into the void.

CHAPTER TWENTY-ONE
Under the Mountain

The only light that penetrated the tunnel was from the narrow opening high above them. The dim glow allowed them to get their bearings on which direction to proceed, but unfortunately, there was a large mound of stones they'd have to climb over before continuing into the tunnel.

"Hurry, climb over these rocks and run inside!" Mas shouted. "I can't be sure we weren't seen entering the shaft."

The boys had scaled several mountains with rocky outcroppings, so they made quick work of climbing and descending to the other side.

"It looks like clear sailing from here," Sam said. He pulled out his blue stone for light and started walking down the tunnel.

"I wouldn't be so sure of that," Mas replied.

Suddenly, they heard a cascade of small stones and boulders falling behind them.

"Run!" Mas yelled.

No sooner had he spoken than a blaze breached the entrance and sent a wave of fire toward the group. Luckily, the pile of stones they'd climbed over blocked the cone of fire, and the only effect of the flames were a few burn marks on Yuma's clothing.

Mas kept pushing everyone to move as fast as possible. The sounds of scraping and falling stones near the entrance of the tunnel meant that something was trying to claw its way in. Then there was silence.

Yuma, who'd been pulling up the rear, told everyone to stand still and listen. They could still hear the tumble of a few stones, but the scraping and digging had stopped.

"It looks like the opening was too small for it to follow us. It must have given up," Yuma said.

Mas shook his head. "I don't believe that it's in its nature to give up."

All of a sudden, they heard a low growl and then an ear-splitting roar, followed by another blast of fire. Fortunately, they had moved far enough into the tunnel that they only felt a wave of heat and saw the light of the flames.

"It looks like we're safe for now," Yuma said.

They knew the blocked entrance would prevent the creature from following them, so the group continued into the narrowing mountain passageway. After hearing another roar far in the distance, they realized they were rid of the beast, at least for now.

For the first few hours, they trudged up an incline. The walls had been roughly hacked by workers from long ago, but the path itself was smooth. Small stones that had fallen from the walls were scattered along the trail, but those were easy to avoid. The blue stones gave them enough light to make their way through the narrow tunnels.

Soon, the incline began to flatten, and walking became easier. Before long, they reached an area where the light from their blue stones was dulled.

"We must have reached an open cavern," Mas said. "The light from our blue stones is being absorbed by the darkness of space. We will only be able to see a short distance in front of us, so stay close."

They could still see parts of the wall that were nearest to them. They realized that this area had not been carved by workers and was a natural part of the cave, probably created by the flow of water that had ended thousands of years ago.

"Which way should we go?" Jeff asked.

"It makes sense that we should keep going in the same direction that we've been traveling," Mas replied.

"But couldn't the exit be in any direction?" Alina asked.

"It could be," Yuma said. "We should split into two groups and search for the opening. I'll take Jeff and Sam. We should stay close so that we can call out and hear each other."

"If you find anything, just yell," Mas said.

"Mas, do you have a flint and stone that we could make a flame with?" Jeff asked.

"Yes, but why do you want that?"

"If we light a small fire, wouldn't the flame follow the draft of air in the tunnel, and shouldn't that lead to the other entrance?" Jeff asked.

"Jeff, that's a brilliant idea," Mas said. "It will also help us see each other better." He pulled out his flint and stone.

Mas started a fire with some dried material and twigs that he kept in his pack for just that reason. Then he separated the burning matter and placed it on two flat stones. He gave one to each group, plus a little more kindling to keep the flames going. Even though the flames were small and gave little warmth, they helped brighten the light of the blue stones.

The fire flickered in all directions, not giving them any indication of where the back entrance could be found. They split up and, after walking a short distance, Yuma called out.

"I think we have something. The draft is pulling our flame in the direction we've been walking."

"Ours too," Alina shouted back.

"The cavern is so big that the exit could still be anywhere. Let's keep walking in that direction and see what happens," Yuma called.

Between the blue stones and the tiny flames, they were all still able to see each other even as they walked further and further away.

"We must be getting closer to the other side of the cave because the draft is really pulling on our flame," Mas yelled.

"So is ours. I can see a gap in the wall," Yuma called back as they walked toward the opening.

"There's another opening over here," Alina shouted. "We're going to see where it leads. Wait there, we'll be back shortly."

The hole that Alina and Mas had found was littered with small bones and rotting carcasses. The stench was terrible. The opening was only large enough for a man to walk through in a crouched position. It was also very narrow, but the direction that the flame flickered showed that it could possibly be a way out.

The further they walked, the more putrid the smell became.

"It smells like something died in here," Mas said, pulling his cloak over his nose.

"I agree. I don't think I can take it any longer," Alina said.

"Let's go back and check out the other opening," Mas said.

As they turned, they heard scraping noises further down the tunnel, which seemed to be getting closer.

"I'm not sure what is making that sound, but I don't want to find out," Mas said. "Let's go back and check out what the others found."

When they reached the rest of the group, they could see by the flame's movement that the draft was stronger there. It could be the tunnel that would lead them out from under the mountain. They followed the direction of the flame for a while longer.

Alina pointed up ahead. "There, I see an opening."

Mas squinted. "I don't see it."

"Follow where I'm pointing. It's very hard to see because it's so dark in here, but there's a slight difference in color. Look, the flame is really pulling hard in that direction. It has to be the way out."

As the group got closer, they could glimpse the opening. Their spirits lifted in the hope that they would soon be out of this dark cave and back into the light, and that's when they saw a deep gorge.

They walked to the edge of the gorge. It wasn't very wide, but it was wide enough to stop them from getting to the opening.

"It's too far to jump across," Mas said.

"I should be able to make it," Yuma said. "We have some rope. I could tie the rope to each side and cross that way."

"That might work, but that would be pretty dangerous. Anyway, there isn't anything to tie the rope to," said Alina, pointing to the other side of the gorge.

"Wait a minute," Sam said, pulling a small bag from his pack. "Eletha gave me this. She said there would come a time when everything seemed lost, and no path existed. She said to spread the sand and it will show the way. Let's try it."

Sam cupped his hand and poured some sand into it. "Here goes nothing," he said as he cast the sand into the open gorge.

The flow of air carried the sand in all directions. At first, nothing happened, and then they noticed something sparkling along the right side of the gorge. It was like seeing stars in the sky on a dark night. The group walked toward the glittering darkness, and to their surprise, there was a narrow path that led to the far side of the gorge. It was just wide enough, if one clung to the wall, for a person to cross.

"It looks like Eletha was right," Mas said.

"Let's go, but be careful," Alina cautioned. "It's very narrow."

"Let me throw all our packs to the other side," Yuma said. "We don't need those strapped to our backs as we cross."

Everyone took off their packs and Yuma threw them across next to the opening, making a small echo throughout the cavern.

"Wow, sound really travels in here," Sam said.

"Speaking of sounds, we heard an odd noise in the other tunnel, and it was coming toward us, so we had better get going," Mas said.

Everyone crossed safely. They picked up their belongings and had just started down the path when Jeff stopped.

"Wait a minute, I forgot one of my small packs," he said.

They all stopped and waited.

Jeff saw his pack, bent down, and picked it up. As he stood and looked across the gorge, he noticed there were four red globes on the other side. They seemed to be floating in mid-air.

"Mas, come here," Jeff said, pointing across the gorge. "Look over there. There are four red globes, and I can't make out what they are."

Suddenly, the red globes separated.

"Those aren't globes," Mas said. "Those are eyes. That would explain the noise Alina and I heard in the tunnel."

Yuma, Alina, and Sam came back to where Mas and Jeff were, wondering what was taking them so long. Mas put his hand to his lips to keep everyone silent. He pointed across the gorge. The red globes shone like beacons in the darkness, and they all saw them immediately. They watched a while longer to see if they could determine what was behind those red balls of fire, but they were still too far away. As they watched, two eyes went to the left and two eyes moved to the right. There was no sound—whatever creature this was, it moved like a hunter. The red eyes kept disappearing and reappearing in a different location, and they were getting closer.

"We had better get out of here," Mas said. "I believe we are being stalked. Quickly, down the tunnel."

They all turned and ran, but they could hear something following them and, whatever it was, it moved fast. The sounds were getting closer, and soon they could hear hissing right behind them. That's when they turned to face their pursuers.

Two young dragons stared at them, baring their teeth, crouched about twenty feet away. They were almost the size of a grown man. Their scaly skin gleamed black with stripes of green running down their backs. A line of bony growths shone down the middle of their spines. Their wings were not fully grown but must have been strong enough to allow them to cross the gorge.

"They are still young and haven't gained the use of fire," Mas said. "Otherwise, they would have already used it. Nonetheless, even at this size, they are quite the adversaries."

"Draw your weapons and back up slowly," Yuma instructed.

Unfortunately, for every step backward the group took, the pair of dragons took two. Without provocation, the dragons suddenly rushed at the group. The first one plowed into Yuma, landing on his chest, snapping his sharp teeth at the soft flesh of Yuma's neck. Fortunately, Yuma was prepared and held the dragon's jaws away by placing his sword against its neck. Normally, given the pressure that he was exerting on the sword, it should have sliced deep into the flesh, but the dragon's scales prevented the sharp blade from doing any damage.

The other dragon charged toward Alina and Mas, snarling and snapping, trying to find a soft piece of flesh to bite. As they backed away, both Mas and Alina slipped on some loose gravel and fell to the ground. They kept jabbing their swords at the creature, trying to keep it away as they struggled to stand. The dragon grabbed Mas's sword in his jaws, yanked it from his hands, and threw it to the side. Then it rammed Alina, sending her flying onto Mas. The dragon stood on its hind legs and prepared to pounce.

Jeff ran toward Mas and Alina with his sword drawn. Sam saw the dragon on top of Yuma and pulled out his bow. He pointed the arrow at the dragon and released his shot.

Yuma's strength was fading. The dragon's jaws were only inches away when an arrow tore through its body. The scream that followed filled the tunnel.

The other dragon heard the cry and wheeled around, only to see Jeff's sword closing in on its neck. The dragon was fast and moved just in time, but not before the sword flew into its shoulder. It too shrieked in pain as it turned and fled down the tunnel.

"Is everyone okay?" Mas asked breathlessly.

"Other than a few bruises, I think we are good," Yuma said.

"That was quick thinking, boys. We owe you our lives," Mas said to Jeff and Sam.

"You would have done the same for us," Jeff said, and they all nodded.

"I can't see how the other dragon would survive, but if it makes it back to the lair, we are going to have one upset mother dragon," Mas told the group. "We may have to deal with her when we reach the other side. We had better get going. I want to get out of this darkness."

Sam quickly went over to the dead dragon to try to retrieve his arrow.

"Jeff, can you help me find my arrow? It should be in the dragon."

"There it is," Alina said, pointing to the wall.

The arrow had not only penetrated the scales of the

dragon but had passed through him and embedded itself into the stone.

"What kind of arrow could do that?" Alina asked.

"I don't know, but let's remember its amazing strength," Mas said.

The group headed down the passageway toward the fresh air that was funneling up through the tunnel. At that moment, they had no idea how much those arrows would play a part in their adventure.

CHAPTER TWENTY-TWO
Into the Green

"We must be getting close to the end," Mas said. "The air is getting much fresher."

Jeff and Sam nodded in agreement, for they had smelled that scent many times when they climbed the White Mountains with their father. The air smelled like a mountain forest, full of the most fragrant evergreen trees imaginable.

Soon a faint light began to filter into the cave. The light became brighter, and they knew that their trek through darkness was nearing an end. Their spirits soared until they reached the end of the passageway where they saw a tangle of roots and thick thorn bushes blocking the exit. Thankfully, the amazing scent was so intoxicating that it gave them a newfound energy. They made quick work of removing the barrier that lay between them and what seemed like paradise.

As they exited, they stood high on a bluff overlooking a valley. A strong breeze streamed down the side of the snow-capped mountain and gave them a chill. Without thinking, they all pulled snug their outer clothing to ward off the cold.

They'd had to shade their eyes after becoming accustomed to the darkness of the cave. Now, as their sight adjusted to the brightness of the day, the most stunning vision appeared before them. The five companions simply stared, for words could not express what they were seeing.

The walls of the valley were covered in broad-leafed trees showing all the possible shades of green. The spring buds on many of the shrubs were blooming in all the colors of the rainbow. A waterfall roared from the highest peak of the surrounding mountains and flowed into a river that snaked its way through the valley and finally emptied into a small lake below them. Even from this distance, they could tell that the water was clear and pure. In the middle of the lake stood an island that radiated a blue glow, a glow that the bluest sky could not equal.

"This is so beautiful. In all my days, I have never seen its match," Alina said.

"Nor have I," Mas agreed.

The group stood and gazed a while longer, unable to pull themselves away from the view until Mas broke the spell.

"Now we must be on our guard, for I fear we have angered the beast that dwells within the mountain," he warned. "She will be more dangerous now. She will be looking for those who slayed her offspring."

Everyone studied the terrain, trying to find the easiest pathway to the valley below. Jeff and Sam explored the small bluff where they stood.

"Sam, look at that," Jeff said, pointing to a group of tall shrubs growing along the mountain wall. The leaves were swaying in a strange way. As Jeff and Sam got nearer to the wall, they could feel a warm breeze filtering through the bushes. They pulled the branches of the shrubs apart and spied an opening in the wall. It appeared to be an archway carved into the mountainside.

"Mas, look at what we found!" Jeff called.

Mas, Alina, and Yuma hurried over to the boys, surprised at what they'd discovered.

"I wonder if this leads to the opening below," Yuma said. "I suppose there is only one way to find out." Yuma began to descend the rock staircase, then stopped and warned the others: "Be careful, the stairs are very steep and slippery. If you tumble, the only thing that will stop you is the bottom."

The darkness was returning, so they all pulled out their blue stones. They were thankful for the constant flow of warm, fresh air rising from below. Without that, the confining space would be suffocating.

"It seems like the air is getting warmer," Sam said.

"We must be getting close to the bottom," Mas replied.

No sooner had Mas spoken than the stairs ended, and they found themselves in a small open space. An archway with a corridor led into another dark passageway.

"It has to lead to the outside," Mas said as they entered another tunnel.

They soon noticed that water was dripping from above and had created a shallow pool within the confines of the corridor.

"I wonder if we are walking under the lake that we saw from above," Mas said.

"We are traveling in that direction, so it would make sense," Alina agreed. "There must be an opening further ahead. Hopefully, it lets us out on the island."

The further they walked, the deeper the water got. It now reached their waists.

"We had better remove our top layers of clothing and try to keep them dry," Alina said. "We won't be able to start a fire to dry anything because I fear the dragon will discover us if we do. With the chill coming off the mountain, we will need warm clothes this night."

Everyone removed some of their outer clothing. The water kept rising. When it finally reached the height of Sam's chin, it leveled off and didn't get any higher. Slowly, the water began to go down and they felt themselves on an upward climb. They continued walking for a while longer until they started to see brightness ahead.

"I think we are coming to the end. I can see some light up ahead," Mas said.

The closer they got to the light, the shallower the water became, until they were walking on a dry, stone surface. Soon they came to a narrow staircase that led upwards. A beautiful blue glow was streaming in, lighting up the area. Now they all knew what was above. The boys, eager to see the forest, put their outer clothing back on and ran up the stairs without waiting for Mas and the others.

Jeff and Sam were the first ones to exit and stand in the forest. The ground was free of branches and other debris that usually littered a forest floor. A soft spongy layer of pine needles and moss muffled their footsteps. It felt like they were walking on air. The trees were not crowded together. Each one had enough room to grow and reach its full height, and they seemed to have been planted by someone. Even though the trees formed a thick canopy a few feet above their heads, the sun's rays filtered through a few open gaps, adding a brilliance to the area's beauty. A stunning view of the lake and forest beyond were visible in every direction. The place was perfect. They all knew that something magical was at work in this forest.

"It is even more magnificent than from the view above," Alina said, and they all nodded in agreement.

Everyone stood lost in the beauty of the surroundings until Sam spoke.

"Where are they?" he asked.

Jeff looked at his brother with puzzlement. "What do you mean?"

"Where are the cones?" Sam said. "There aren't any on the ground, and I can't see any in the trees."

Suddenly, the reality of the situation hit all of them at once and they remembered why they were there. They shook themselves from their reveries, realizing what they had to do.

"The cones must grow near the tops of the trees," Mas said. "We need to climb up and see if they are growing above. Once we know that, then we'll figure out how to pluck them from the trees."

"Sam and I will go," Jeff said. "We're the smallest and we're good tree climbers."

Mas opened his pack and pulled out two sacks with shoulder straps, not much bigger than small grocery bags. "Here is one for each of you. Place the straps around your neck and under your arm. When you grab the cones, put them in the sacks so you can use your hands to maneuver through the canopy. We should try to get two full sacks in case something happens and we lose some on the journey back. We want to make sure we have enough to save the Princess. Now go, but be careful. It's getting dark and soon the sun will set."

Jeff and Sam each climbed a different tree. Getting through the thick covering to where the cones grew was difficult. Eventually, with only a few scrapes and cuts, the boys penetrated the canopy and popped their heads into the clearing above.

"Do you see anything?" Mas called from below.

"Yes, I see them. They're everywhere, but they're spread apart," Jeff shouted as he pulled himself onto the layer of thick evergreen branches. He turned to Sam. "I think if we do the crawl that Dad taught us to do on thin ice, the branches will support us. Let me try it first. I'm heavier and if they hold me, they should hold you."

Jeff spread his body on top of the canopy and then inched his way forward. When he was satisfied that the tops of the trees could support him, he let Sam know that he could start his search.

The boys found that if they were careful and avoided some small openings in the canopy, they were able to crawl along the tops of the trees without falling through. They grabbed a number of cones and put them in their sacks.

"Sam, I see a cluster of cones," Jeff said. "If I can get those, we should have enough. I'm going to try and reach them."

Jeff pulled himself along the top and, just as he grasped the first cone, he felt himself sink and fall into the branches. Sam saw him disappear into the canopy and was terrified.

"Jeff, are you okay?" Sam yelled.

When he didn't get a reply, he quickly found a thin part of the covering and descended under the canopy. He saw Jeff dangling from his sack, which had caught on a branch, saving him from falling to the ground. Mas and Yuma were climbing up the tree to pull him to safety.

"Are you okay?" Sam yelled again.

"Yes, and thank goodness for the sack," Jeff said with a smile as they all safely reached the forest floor.

Mas looked in the boys' sacks, counting the cones. "I don't think we've gathered enough cones, and now it's getting dark. As much as I hate to, I think we should wait and try more foraging in the morning. We should be safe here tonight. Even the dragon's eyes couldn't penetrate this canopy."

"I agree, but we should sleep near the stone entrance," Yuma said. "If we need to make a quick exit, we can run into the passageway."

Thankfully, they all had dry clothing to wrap themselves in, for the chill came in as swiftly as the darkness. Something about this place made them feel safe and secure, so the group settled down and fell fast asleep. The spongy floor of the forest was an added benefit, for it was the softest thing they'd slept on since they'd left the Garish dwelling.

CHAPTER TWENTY-THREE
Morning Has Risen

Sam turned over to avoid the beam of light that was shining on his face. He opened his eyes slightly and saw Jeff staring up at the canopy, eyes wide open.

"You're awake," Sam whispered, noticing that their other three companions were still sleeping.

"I just woke up. What a great sleep," Jeff said. "I was staring at the canopy, trying to remember where that large cluster of cones was. If I can just find them, we'll have enough so that we can start our journey back. I'm starting to miss home. How about you?"

"Yeah, I am too," Sam answered.

The boys continued to stare into the canopy, both seemingly lost in their own worlds. The soft rays of the sun streamed through the trees and warmed their bodies, almost putting them back to sleep, and that's when they heard the sound.

It was faint at first, hard to distinguish between the dull roar of the distant waterfall and the rustling of the tree branches. But this was a different sound, not one created by nature.

As they listened, they could tell that it was getting closer. Then, nothing. The boys knew that something was different, and that they had better wake their companions. As they gently shook their friends awake, the sun's rays disappeared, and they heard a loud whoosh slightly above the canopy. The branches moved above as the sound became faint and the sun reappeared.

Mas, Alina, and Yuma woke up, and they knew immediately what had caused the noise. Mas put his hand up to his mouth to signal everyone to stay silent. No one moved. Then from far away, they heard it—a screech so loud that even from this distance, they had to cover their ears. It was a pained scream, a scream that made the five of them shudder. Again, the rushing wind came and, although it caused a ripple in the canopy, it was at the far edge of the forest.

They sat there in silence, nervously waiting and wondering if something more terrifying was going to happen. After a couple of minutes, Mas stood up and edged his way to the outer border of the forest to peer into the sky. Clouds were moving in from the West, but beyond that, the heavens were clear and, as far as he could see, any threat was gone.

"What was that?" Sam asked as Mas returned to the group.

"That, my friends, was a dragon, and she is hunting for us," Mas said. "We had better hurry. Let's get the remaining cones and leave." He pointed to the sacks that were placed near the opening of the passageway. "I combined the cones into two sacks. We only need another half a sack to ensure that we have enough."

Jeff went over and grabbed the half-full sack, putting it around his neck and under his arm. "I think I know approximately where the cluster of cones is. There are enough in that one spot to fill this sack, so there isn't any reason for both of us to go above."

"Jeff is right," Yuma said. "Let's get everything ready to make a quick exit. If the dragon is watching us, we'll need to move fast."

Except for their weapons, they placed their belongings next to the opening that led to the tunnel below.

Jeff began to climb up one of the trees. He'd almost reached the top of the canopy when Alina called out and told him to stop. She'd noticed that the sun's rays no longer warmed the forest floor. She ran to the outer edge of the forest, looked up, and realized that clouds had blanketed the sky.

Alina rushed back to the group and shouted up to Jeff. "Jeff, the clouds cover the sky, but the creature has dragon-sight, which gives her the ability to see through them. We will not be able to see her until she is close. You must be quick!"

"I will be!" Jeff called back as he poked his head above the trees.

He spotted the cluster about twenty feet from where he stood. He decided to go back below the canopy and climb his way through the undergrowth, which would shorten his time in the open. Climbing through this part of the forest was very difficult. The trees were thick, which explained the large cluster of cones. After many scrapes to his hands and face, Jeff determined that he was in approximately the right spot. He nudged his body through the upper branches and when he popped his head out of the canopy, he realized that he had come up in the middle of the cluster. He filled most of the sack by reaching through the branches and staying below the canopy, but he still needed more. He quickly poked his head up through the canopy and saw another group of cones about five feet from where he hung. He went below and tried climbing through the tangle of branches, but he had to give up. It was impenetrable.

"Jeff, are you almost done?" Alina called.

"I'm just about full. There's one more cluster close to me but I can't reach them from below. I have to go onto the canopy." Jeff made his way back to an opening and called to the group below, "Can you see or hear anything?"

Yuma had been near the edge of the forest watching for the slightest movement in the sky. He motioned to the others that he couldn't see anything.

"Yuma says there isn't anything that he can see," Mas shouted.

"Okay, I'm going up," Jeff called as he climbed out onto the canopy.

The spot was so full of cones that he was able to swiftly fill up his sack. But then, he heard a loud screech from above.

"Quickly, Jeff, get down! You've been seen!" Alina yelled.

Jeff panicked as he tried to get through the thickest part of the canopy. He twisted and squirmed his way below the top of the trees but kept getting stuck in the branches. The screams from above were getting louder and his companions kept yelling to go faster. But the harder he tried, the more entangled he became. Finally, he gave one big push to get him through the tightest branches, but then he realized that his sack had become caught and he couldn't unwrap it from around his neck.

Suddenly, a blast of fire penetrated the forest, narrowly missing the group.

"Cut the cord and release yourself!" Mas yelled.

"I can't leave the cones!" Jeff yelled back.

"You have to!" Mas shouted as a second blast of heat scorched the area near the tunnel.

Finally, Jeff pulled his sword out and cut the cord. He fell from the trees to the soft ground below, leaving his bag of cones stuck high above.

The group ran for the cover of the tunnel. When they got close, they saw that the dragon's final blast of fire had burned all but a few vital supplies. But worst of all, the sacks of cones were destroyed.

As they entered the pathway, they turned to see a wave of fire coming toward them. They rushed into the darkness of the passage, where they could still feel the heat from the explosions of fire. They fled further and further into the tunnel, knowing the dragon could not reach them. But even deep within the passageway, they could hear the continued blasts of fire that the dragon rained upon the forest above.

When the savagery and wrath of the dragon had finally turned to silence, the group slowly came up the stairs, hoping to retrieve any cones that may have survived. What they saw was total devastation. Every tree had been burnt to the ground, leaving only smoldering stumps. They all just stared, with tears in their eyes, at the destruction of this once-perfect forest. In their hearts, each of them knew what this meant to their world.

"We have to be able to do something," Jeff said.

"I am sorry, but as you can see, it is all gone," Yuma said. "There is nothing left. We must go before the dragon comes back."

They turned to leave, but then Sam yelled, "No, maybe there are some cones buried below the surface. We have to try!"

Jeff and Sam left the protection of the passageway, venturing out into the middle of the burnt forest. They both started to dig below the ground to see if they could find any buried cones.

After a while, Alina came to the boys and held them close. "I am sorry, boys, but they are gone. We must leave," she said soothingly.

At that point, they knew their search was futile.

"But we came all this way, and we were so close to saving the Princess and your world," Jeff said.

"I know, but the dragon's fire was so intense that it burnt everything far below the surface. Nothing escaped the rage of this creature," Alina said as Mas and Yuma joined them.

With that understanding, more tears flowed. They slowly headed back toward the tunnel, and that's when they heard a thunderous screech from above.

Out of the clouds flew the dragon, full of fury. Her red eyes saw only one thing: the people who had slain her offspring.

"Run!" Mas yelled.

The group ran toward the cover of the passageway. As they reached the entrance, Mas realized Jeff hadn't come with them. He still stood in the burnt forest, staring into the sky, facing the dragon, sword in hand.

"Jeff, what are you doing? Get back here now!" cried Mas.

Sam tried to squirm past Yuma and Alina to reach Jeff, but they caught him and held him tight.

A rage was developing deep within Jeff's heart. A rage of injustice. So many people had perished because of the brutality and mercilessness of this dragon. And now that it had destroyed the cones and the magical forest, the Princess would die, and with her, so would Alfham.

Mas kept calling for him to return, but Jeff stood his ground, staring defiantly at the dragon. Finally, Mas ran toward Jeff to bring him back. He stumbled into a small hole and fell to the ground. Mas reeled in pain, unable to stand.

The dragon was getting closer when another scream was heard high in the sky. Windsong flew through the clouds, heading directly at the dragon. The dragon momentarily altered her flight to face the eagle, but before she could spew a stream of fire, Windsong attacked. Windsong tried to tear at the dragon's eyes with his sharp talons, but the dragon swung her long neck and hit the eagle, causing it to flutter to the ground. The dragon continued her flight toward Jeff.

"We have a chance to save Jeff and Mas! Sam, you stay here!" Alina cried.

She and Yuma grabbed their weapons and hurried toward Jeff and Mas. Sam grabbed his bow and ran after them.

Yuma and Alina reached Mas and helped him to his feet just as they saw Sam race by them to join Jeff.

"Sam, come back!" Alina yelled as she and Yuma helped Mas back to the tunnel.

Now both boys stood in the middle of the burnt forest, bow drawn and sword at the ready as the dragon headed straight at them.

She was close when Sam released his first arrow. With the arrogance and conviction that nothing could stop her, the dragon ignored the arrow flying toward her chest. But when it penetrated her breast and tore away the scale that protected her heart, she screamed in pain, and a fear that she had never felt before raced through her body. She stopped and hovered high above the boys. Then she saw Sam grab an arrow and ready his bow for another shot.

This increased the rage of the dragon, for as long as she had been alive, no one had ever dared stand up to her.

"We have one shot at this, Sam. Aim for her heart," Jeff said.

Evil, cruelty, and hatred radiated from the dragon's red eyes as she plunged toward them.

Jeff and Sam held their ground.

The dragon landed on top of the tunnel entrance. Alina and Yuma were just able to move Mas out of the way before the doorway partially collapsed, preventing them from helping Jeff and Sam. She crouched between them and the tunnel. There was no way to escape. Jeff and Sam had to fight.

The dragon lifted her head and roared a cold-blooded cry into the sky. Then she took a step toward them, her eyes piercing into their very beings.

Sam notched a black-tipped arrow and Jeff readied his sword, fear rushing through their bodies.

Then the dragon inhaled.

"Now!" Jeff cried.

Jeff threw his sword as hard as he had ever thrown anything in his life, while Sam released his arrow. The dragon, remembering the sting from Sam's first arrow, barely avoided the shot, but Jeff's throw was true. The sword penetrated deep into the dragon's breast to where her heart beat. Only the hilt of the sword showed. She looked down at her chest and grasped the hilt with her teeth, drawing the sword from her body and throwing it to the ground.

"She still lives!" Sam yelled.

The dragon turned toward the boys and tried to inhale, but her breath would not come, and without breath, her fire was extinguished. She flew into the air, her red eyes glaring at the boys. Then she turned and flew toward the safety of her mountain. She hadn't traveled far when a horrible sound came from deep within her. A sound of pain, a sound of defeat, and then she fell to the ground, crashing into the side of the mountain, never to kill again.

CHAPTER TWENTY-FOUR
Rebirth

Mas, Yuma, and Alina ran toward the boys, grabbing and hugging them, and making sure they weren't hurt.

"Are you okay?" Alina asked.

"Yes, I am," Jeff said.

"Me too," Sam added.

Once the group confirmed that they were all fine, they gazed at their surroundings. The impact of the dragon hitting the ground was tremendous, for her body had penetrated the side of the mountain. The only part showing was her enormous head and her open red eyes, which no longer showed life or rage. But even with the death of the dragon, none of them felt joy. The hills had lost the vivid colors that had painted the sides of the valley. The dragon had ended that with her fiery breath. Everywhere they looked, they encountered a charred landscape, and they knew what that meant for this world.

After a while and many spent tears, Mas spoke. "We can ask ourselves—how could this happen? We were so close and there was so much at stake. We can only be satisfied that we gave everything we had, and that truth is the only thing we can take back with us. We can't give up. We must go back and try to make our world better."

They all nodded in agreement as they turned and walked toward the passageway. After picking up the few items that the dragon hadn't destroyed, they headed back into the darkness of the tunnel, the beginning of the path that led home.

"Does everyone have their blue stones?" Mas asked as he grabbed his stone from his pouch.

Alina, Yuma, and Jeff held up their stones and a blue glow lit up the area.

"I can't find mine," Sam said, searching through the small sack tied to his waist. "I thought I put it in with my vial. I know I have it. Maybe it's in my sweatshirt pocket."

He reached into his front pocket, but then pulled his hand out quickly. "Ouch, something jabbed me." He carefully reached into his pocket again, and this time pulled out a small pinecone.

"What's that doing in your pocket?" Jeff asked.

"I don't know." Sam looked at Jeff, and then he realized what it was and why it was there. "Jeff, do you remember when we brought the Christmas tree into the house and we heard something fall, but we couldn't see what it was? It must have been the cone. Before we went to bed, I went downstairs to get my Beanie Baby off the couch and that's when I noticed the cone under the table."

"But why is it in your sweatshirt pocket?" Jeff asked.

"I just put it there and then ran upstairs to bed," Sam said. "I forgot all about it. This is the cone that was on the tree. Do you remember what Azar said about the first cone that the tree produces? I wonder ..."

"Could it be?" Jeff asked.

Both boys turned and raced out of the tunnel back into the charred forest. They ran into the middle of the island. Sam held the cone in his hand, waiting for something to happen.

Mas, Alina, and Yuma wondered what they were doing and came after them.

"What's going on here?" Mas asked.

"In our world, a man gave us a Christmas tree, and the cone that Sam found in his sweatshirt was from that tree," Jeff explained. "Our tree radiated a bluish glow like the ones that were here, so we think the cone may be from the same type of tree. The man told us that the cone has special seeds."

Even with the explanation, Mas, Yuma, and Alina were confused as to what was supposed to happen.

"This needs to work," Sam kept saying as the minutes ticked away. "There is no way we came all this way for nothing. Come on, something needs to happen."

"Sam, try putting the cone on the ground," Jeff suggested.

"Good idea," Sam said. As he slowly bent down, the cone started to vibrate in his hands, and when he placed it on the ground, the cone opened like a rose in bloom. There, sitting on the charred floor of the forest, were hundreds of seeds.

"It opened!" Alina exclaimed.

"Now we have to plant them," Sam said.

"Let's plant one and see how big it gets, then we can plant the rest," Jeff said.

Sam brushed away the burnt matter and dug until he reached the dark, healthy soil below. He placed one seed into the ground and covered it with more dirt. Then he waited.

"Nothing is happening," Sam said with disappointment.

"Maybe it takes more time than we think," Jeff said.

The longer they waited, the more anxious everyone became.

"Sam, maybe we need to water it," Jeff said. "Try putting some liquid from the small vial on it."

Sam reached into his pouch and pulled out the small crystal bottle. He placed a single drop of fluid onto the spot where he'd planted the seed. Immediately, the area turned the most beautiful shade of blue and the ground started to vibrate.

The group slowly backed away, and that's when it happened: a small, green sprout pushed through the dirt, and then, with a speed that none of them could believe, a full tree burst through the ground, reaching up toward the sky.

They all stared at the tree in shock. At the very top, more cones than they could even count sprouted from the branches.

"The tree and the cones look just like the ones that were here before," Yuma said with a wide smile.

"Do you know what this means?" Alina asked excitedly.

"I believe we do," Mas said as the rest of the group nodded in agreement. "Jeff, climb up and pick every cone that you can. We don't need any more cones than what's on this one tree."

"While Jeff gets the cones, I'm going to keep planting more seeds," Sam said.

"Let's all help," Mas said. "Maybe we can get the forest back to the way it was when we arrived."

Mas, Yuma, and Alina each took seeds and, as they planted them, Sam placed a drop of fluid on each one. By the time Jeff had climbed the tree, picked the cones, and dropped them to the ground, the group had planted many more trees. When they finally finished, they were looking at a beautiful, glowing forest.

"Now that is a sight to behold," Yuma said.

"Whew, that was close! I thought I was going to run out of fluid," Sam said, holding up the vial. "I only have one drop left."

"I'm done!" Jeff yelled as he climbed down the tree.

The group gathered under the tree and collected all the cones into one pile. Alina and Yuma pulled off their outer cloaks and tied the arms together, creating two large pouches.

"Well, what are we waiting for?" Mas said, smiling at everyone. "Let's get these cones picked up and get them back to save the Princess!"

"Mas, how many days have we been traveling?" Jeff asked.

"I believe it's been about nine days," Mas replied.

"So, if it takes another nine to get back to the King's palace, it may be too late to save the Princess," Jeff said. "Why don't we send a big pouch of cones back home with Windsong? It would only take him a day or two. I think the quicker we get these back, the better the chance of curing the Princess. Don't you agree?"

Mas, Alina, and Yuma all looked at each other and nodded their heads, marveling at Jeff's suggestion.

"That's a great idea, and I can't believe I didn't think of

it!" Mas said. He grabbed his whistle and blew into it as hard as he could.

A moment later, they heard a screech coming from high in the sky. Mas held out his arm, and soon, Windsong landed. Mas spoke in the language of the past, with a high pitch, a turn of his head, and several guttural sounds. Windsong squawked and made a low cry, turned his head once, then twice, seeming to acknowledge his task.

Windsong hopped onto the homemade sack of cones and grabbed it with his sharp talons. With a screech and a flap of his huge wings, the eagle was airborne, heading south.

The group stood in silence watching Windsong fly higher and further into the sky until, finally, they lost sight of him.

"We should head home," Mas said, "but it's almost dark and the forest is so beautiful. I think we should camp here tonight, have a hot meal, and leave at first light."

"I think that would be wonderful," Yuma said, and the others nodded.

They ate their meal, then settled down for a good night's sleep, happy with what they'd accomplished.

At first light the next morning, they packed up their gear and grabbed the extra cones.

"I guess it's time to go home," Mas said with a smile. With that, they all headed toward the tunnel.

Jeff turned back to look at the forest and valley one last time. "Mas, do you think this area will ever be the same as it was?"

"With time, nature always repairs itself, and if we save Princess Iris, I am sure that it will. In any case, with the planting of the trees, we've given it a good start," Mas said.

"Yeah, I guess we did," Jeff said as they entered the tunnel that would lead them home.

CHAPTER TWENTY-FIVE

To the Palace

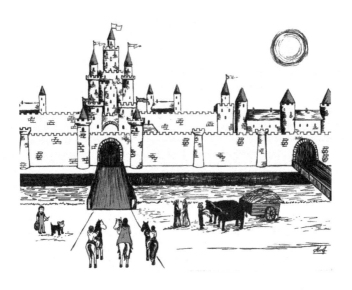

Pejew met the group at the edge of the forest. They could see that he was healed and in good spirits, and that their horses were fully rested.

"I see that you were able to retrieve the cones," Pejew said.

"Yes, Windsong is carrying a bag to the palace," Mas said. He told Pejew what had happened and how Jeff and Sam defeated the dragon.

"You two are quite the young men," Pejew said to the boys.

"Yes, they are," Alina said, and Mas and Yuma nodded in agreement.

"If we could, we would spend some more time with you, but we must be on our way," Mas said. "In case Windsong doesn't make it back with the cones, we must take them."

"I understand. I think you will find your trip through the Wood a little less challenging this time," Pejew said.

The creatures of the forest had known immediately that there was a new Master of the Wood. Their ability to understand the slightest changes in their world was far more advanced than man's. The darkness they had been living under had been lifted and most of them welcomed this change, for now they could come out of hiding. As in everything, there were those who relished evil and chaos, but they moved deep into the forest, never to be heard from again. The Wood was at peace.

"Ride as hard as you will, for nothing in this forest will bother you. I have seen to that," Pejew said.

"We all thank you," Mas said.

With that, they mounted their horses, waved goodbye to Pejew, and headed deep into the Wood. Just as Pejew had told them, they passed through the forest without delay. By pushing their horses, they managed to exit the forest by nightfall.

"Our home, the Garish dwelling, is close," Alina told Mas and the boys. "It would be best if you spent the night there with us and rested the horses. That way, they will be fresh, and you can leave at first light."

They spent a restful night at the Garish dwelling. In the morning, they said their goodbyes to Yuma, Alina, and their friends.

"Thank you for everything you have done for us," Mas said to the Garish people. "Without you, we would never have succeeded in our quest."

"Oh yes, one last thing," Yuma said. "You won't have to worry about the Boitus on your trip home. After you left, my clan gave them quite the send-off. I don't think the Boitus will ever be coming near these canyons again."

Yuma led Mas and the boys through the dark tunnels of the Garish dwelling. "We will let you out on the southern wall," Yuma said. "That will cut another day off your journey."

When Yuma opened the door, the brightness of the sun blinded them, but they welcomed its warmth. They said a final goodbye to Yuma, then mounted their horses and entered the Plains of Drun. It was there that they noticed a slight change in their surroundings. The seemingly dead grass plains they had passed through on their previous journey north now showed green at the roots. They realized the grass was starting to grow and the insects that usually populate the fields were buzzing everywhere.

"Well, this is definitely a good sign," Mas said to the boys as they continued to travel south.

When they reached the woodlands where they had first entered this world, the trees that had looked dead before now boasted small red and green buds popping from their branches. They saw birds flying in all directions, calling to their partners and singing happy songs. Chipmunks and squirrels ran along the ground trying to uncover treats that had been hidden long ago.

"I think Windsong must have made it back with the cones, for something here has definitely changed," Mas said.

"I know, everything looked dead when we first arrived, and now life seems to be returning," Jeff replied. "Could it really have changed that fast?"

"Unless our eyes deceive us, I believe that it has," Mas said.

They traveled through wooded areas interspersed with grassy fields and slow-running brooks until they reached a wide, dirt road that would lead them to the King's palace.

Once they left the forest, large fields appeared on both sides of the road. As they crested a small hill, they could see the walled city of Nysium, the home of King Olim, Queen Arual, and Princess Iris. Walls as high as five men stretched far to the east and to the west, seeming to go on forever. A waterway ran all along the wall. The only access points to the city were two big bridges spanning the river, protected day and night by guard towers. Even from this distance, the walled city was amazing, but the most remarkable sight was what rose from its center: a golden castle with towers that reached to the sky.

As Mas and the boys got closer to the city, they spotted growing fields spread for as far as the eye could see, full of people tilling and planting the land. A city this size would need an abundance of food to feed the population. In other areas, men were tending herds of very thin oxen.

"This is another good sign," Mas told the boys. "When I left to find you in your world, the people here had all but abandoned these fields and their animals."

Mas saw that Jeff and Sam had become very quiet and were whispering to each other. "What's wrong? You should be happy!"

"We are, but we've never seen a king or met a princess," Sam said. "What should we say and do? They don't know who we are. Do you think they will even agree to meet us?"

Mas looked at Jeff and Sam and smiled. "My two brave boys, by the looks of everything here, you have saved Princess Iris and, in doing that, you have saved Alfham. I think that when the King, Queen, Princess, and their court see you, they will surely know who you are."

The boys noticed something peculiar as they got closer to the gates. The people in the fields stopped working. The men pushing their barges along the river held their place. The guards along the wall stood still and gazed out onto the road.

Jeff looked around. "Mas, they're all staring at us."

Suddenly, as if on cue, everyone erupted into the loudest, most glorious cheers the boys had ever heard and began racing toward them. The gates to the city flew open and there stood King Olim and Queen Arual.

Mas looked at the boys and said with a smile and a wink, "I guess they know who you are."

CHAPTER TWENTY-SIX
Meeting the Princess

Mas, Jeff, and Sam walked through the streets of
the city. The main avenue that led to the castle
was wide and full of people. They passed shops, inns, out-
door eateries, and homes, all to the stare of the crowds.
When they reached the King's castle, the gates were lifted,
and they entered the court area.

There they saw people tending to all kinds of chores,
but when the King and Queen entered, everyone stopped
what they were doing and let them pass.

Mas and the boys walked into the main hall, where colorful banners hung from the walls. On both sides of the room, large fireplaces with blazing fires warmed the hall. The King's advisors and courtiers were already present and lined the outer edges of the room. The King and Queen stepped forward and sat down on their thrones. Next to the Queen's throne was a smaller seat, still empty. Mas, Jeff, and Sam stood in the front of the hall, facing the thrones.

"The King and the Queen don't look very happy, and where is the Princess?" Sam whispered.

"I know, they look sad," Jeff said. "I wonder where she is."

Once the King and Queen were settled, a man with a long, white beard sitting behind and to the left of the King stood up.

"Jeff, he looks just like the man who gave us the tree," Sam said.

"I think you're right," Jeff said in amazement. "It's Azar!"

Mas waved for Jeff and Sam to listen as Azar began to speak.

"Our world is healing. The fields are growing. There is new growth on the trees, and the spirit of our people has returned after a very black period in our world. We have two young boys and one of our own here to thank for this." The man waved for Mas and the boys to come forward, to loud applause from the crowd.

The trio walked up to stand in front of the thrones as the man continued his speech.

"Even though we see that things are getting better, this veil of darkness has not been fully lifted," he said.

Without thinking, Jeff spoke. "Aren't you ...," but before Jeff could finish, the man nodded.

"Yes, I am Azar, the one who gave you the special tree. It is nice to see you again." And to the King and Queen, Azar said, "This is Jefrus and Samion, the boys the ancient legend predicted would come to save our world."

Mas motioned for the boys to bow, and they did so awkwardly.

"Welcome, Jefrus and Samion," King Olim said. "We are indebted to you for everything you've done for us."

"Yes," said Queen Arual. "We are honored to have you here. You've been very brave."

"Thank you, but where is the Princess?" Sam blurted out.

The Queen stood. "Sam, the Princess still sleeps. Her body has healed and that is why our world is healing, but if she does not wake, I am afraid that all will be lost."

"Oh no! Can we see her?" Sam asked.

"Of course you can see her. We would be most honored," Queen Arual said.

The group left the main hall and walked to Princess Iris's room, where the walls were covered in gorgeous tapestries of nature. Small trees were placed around the room, and beautiful birds flaunted their colors and pleasing calls from gilded cages. A door at one end led out to a huge balcony overlooking picturesque gardens, and everything in the Princess's room showed her love for the natural world. In a large bed in front of the balcony doors lay the Princess.

The Queen and Azar brought Jeff and Sam over to her, while King Olim and Mas waited by the door.

Princess Iris had beautiful, long, black hair and an angelic face. Her hands were folded over her white gown and moved slightly with the slow rhythm of her breathing. The Princess's beauty captivated the boys. They couldn't take their eyes off her.

"Will she ever wake up?" Sam asked Azar.

"We have been working day and night since we first treated her," Azar said. "We thought we had cured her because she responded well and her body recovered, but still, she doesn't wake. Something is missing, but we don't know what it is."

"Isn't there anything we can do?" Jeff asked.

"I am afraid not. It's now up to her," Azar said.

Everyone stood silently, observing the sleeping Princess.

Queen Arual looked upset at seeing her daughter in this condition, and said, "We must leave her now."

Azar, Jeff, and the Queen turned to walk out of the room, but Sam stayed, looking down at the Princess. He put his hand in hers. Her hand was warm and soft to the touch. In that touch, Sam was reminded of something important, something very important, but it wouldn't come to him.

"Come on Sam, we have to leave," Jeff called.

Sam let go of the Princess's hand and started walking toward the door when it hit him. He ran back to the Princess, and from the pouch that hung around his waist, he pulled out the small vial of liquid.

"What are you doing?" Azar asked as they all went back to the Princess's bedside.

"On our journey, the dragon burnt the trees that held the cones that we were going to bring back to save the Princess," Sam explained. "We thought that all was lost, but then I found a cone in my pocket, just like the ones the dragon had destroyed. We planted the seeds in the hopes that they would grow into trees. If they grew, we knew that they would produce cones and seeds to help save the Princess. Nothing happened until I placed a drop of liquid from this vial onto the ground where the seed was planted. Like magic, a live tree grew right before our eyes." Sam gazed around at the group with hope in his eyes. "Maybe this elixir will do the same for Princess Iris."

Azar looked at the Queen. The Queen looked at Sam and nodded her approval.

Sam gently placed the last drop of liquid from the crystal vial onto the Princess's lips. For what seemed like an eternity, nothing happened, then suddenly, she took a deep breath.

"Wait, something is happening," the Queen said.

The Princess's fingers twitched, and she reached out and grabbed Jeff's and Sam's hands. Then she opened her eyes.

"Jefrus and Samion, I knew you would come."

CHAPTER TWENTY-SEVEN
Homeward Bound

T

wo days after the Princess had woken, the King put out a proclamation to his people to gather at the gates of the palace to hear an announcement. Thousands gathered in anticipation, for even though their world was healing, there were rumors that the Princess had not yet fully recovered. The King and Queen walked out to the balcony which overlooked the gates and lands beyond.

"As you know, our world had turned bleak," King Olim told the crowd. "Then our saving light, Princess Iris, fell into a deep sleep, turning our world even darker. But that light now shines," the King said as Princess Iris stepped out onto the balcony to an uproar of applause.

When the applause stopped, the King continued. "Here are those who saved her, and in saving her, they have saved all of us."

Mas, Jeff, and Sam walked out onto the balcony and stood next to Princess Iris. This time the cheers and applause did not stop for a long time.

Finally, the King put up his hands to silence the crowd. "To honor the people who have saved our kingdom, in two days' time, there will be feasting throughout the land." Cheering erupted again as the King left the balcony and went back inside.

On the night of the banquet, Jeff, Sam, and Mas sat at the table of honor with King Olim, Queen Arual, Princess Iris, and Azar, surrounded by over two hundred courtiers and dignitaries. A cloud had been lifted from their world and everyone felt lighter, and it showed in the way they were celebrating. It was so loud in the banquet hall that it was hard to hear the person speaking next to them. However, Jeff and Sam still managed to have many conversations about the world they would shortly be leaving.

Jeff went over and sat next to Azar. "I've been thinking: when you were in our world, why didn't you take the cone off the tree, bring it back here, and plant it? You would have had plenty of seeds to cure the Princess."

Azar smiled. "That's very perceptive of you. You see, it wasn't only the seeds that were important in saving the Princess, but where they were grown. That island is magical. There is nothing like it in all of the other worlds. It gives life, and so the seeds pulled that life from the land."

"So why did she need the elixir to wake her up?" Jeff asked.

"That's a good question," Azar said. "The bottle is very old. We believe it is from an ancient Elvish civilization, long gone from this world. I don't know how the elixir survived this long, but whatever it was, it contained something very special. But, since it is all gone, we may never know what it was."

Jeff nodded. "And what are you going to do with the extra seeds that we took from the mountain?"

"We intend to plant them throughout the kingdom to grow the special trees that once filled our land. We hope this will remind our people of the fragility of our world and that they should become better caretakers of it."

"That's a great idea," Jeff said.

Sam sat next to the Princess and spent most of his time speaking with her. The Princess proved to be everything they had said she would be. She was kind, caring, generous, and most of all, magical. In the few days that Jeff and Sam had spent with Princess Iris, they had taken many walks. They had seen her touch a branch of a dead tree and bring it back to life. They had seen birds and small wild animals flock to her side, just to be near her. Sam and Jeff had no doubt that she would save this world.

As the night wore on and the conversation slowed, the boys looked around the room and became very quiet. The Princess noticed this immediately.

"You know, they tell me I was asleep for four full moon cycles," she said. "Only through the care of the wizards and my family was I able to stay alive. I can't imagine how they felt knowing that I might never wake up. Family is everything. How long have you been in our world, away from your family?"

"I don't remember, but it's been a lot of days," Sam said.

"You must be missing your family and your home," the Princess said gently.

"Yes, it was Christmas Eve when we left," Sam told her. "That's a very special time in our world, but mostly, we miss our parents."

Jeff nodded in agreement.

"I know how precious family is. It is time for you to return to your home," the Princess said. She stood and the room became silent.

"Our friends must leave us, and for their great courage

and sacrifice, our world will be forever grateful," the Princess announced. Then she bowed to the boys, and so did everyone in the banquet hall. The night was over.

In the morning, the boys had one last meal and said their goodbyes to King Olim, Queen Arual, and Princess Iris.

"We will never forget you," Princess Iris said, and gave them each a warm hug.

They rode away from the palace with Mas, waving back to their friends. By nightfall, they had arrived at the place where they'd first started their journey. They hastened up the slope to the top of the bluff, where they saw the large tree trunk through which they had first entered this world. The boys dismounted from their horses and walked over to the tree.

"What should we do with our weapons?" Jeff asked Mas.

"I will bring them back to the palace, where they will be kept," Mas said. "They are very special. You are their masters and only you shall wield them. If you ever come back to our world, they will be secured at the King's palace."

"Wait a minute, we should give them names," Jeff said.

"Good idea," Sam agreed.

"I will call my sword 'Dragon Blade,'" Jeff said.

"That's an excellent name," Mas said.

"And I will name my bow 'Dragon Slayer,'" Sam said.

Jeff smiled. "Oh, I like that."

"I think both names are perfect," Mas said as the boys handed him their weapons.

"Okay, now how do we get back?" Sam asked.

"The same way that you came in," Mas said. "Just keep crawling as far as you can, and the tree will take care of the rest." He stopped and grabbed a pouch from his waist. "I have something to give you, for without it, your parents would definitely not be happy with me."

Mas handed the boys the pouch. "When you get back and climb down the tree, you must each take a handful of this dust and blow it on each other. It will bring you to your normal size."

Then Mas gave the boys a hug and wiped a tear from his eye. "I will never forget you two."

"We won't forget you either," Jeff and Sam said as they returned his hug.

"One more thing," Mas said. "I have a parting gift for each of you." He placed a small whistle into each boy's hand, like the one he'd used to call the eagle. "These whistles will be our connection. If you ever need my help, all you'll need to do is blow the whistle. It won't make a sound, but I will surely hear it, and I will come to your aid."

"And if your world ever needs us again and you blow into the whistle, will we hear it?" Jeff asked.

"Yes, you will hear it," Mas said.

"Then I will come and help you," Jeff said.

Sam nodded. "So will I."

The boys gave Mas one last hug and entered the trunk

of the tree. Before going too far, they both turned around and said their last goodbye to Alfham. Then they edged their way into the darkness, using the light of the two moons to show them the way. They kept inching forward until the light was gone.

"How much further do you think it is?" Sam asked.

"I don't know, but Mas told us to just keep going," Jeff said. "Slide up next to me so we are near each other."

It was a tight squeeze, but the boys managed.

"I'm going to miss this place," Sam said. "It was quite the adventure."

"Yes, it was," Jeff replied.

Suddenly, they were both lifted into the air. As they traveled upward, they could see a light above them, and before they knew it, they'd landed at the door that led them home.

They stood at the top of the tree and gazed out over the living room. The moon's light filtered in through the curtained windows, and the odor of the fire still lingered as the last coals burned out. Jeff stared at the clock that hung in the corner of the room.

"Look, Sam, it's only four in the morning. We didn't miss Christmas!"

"It sure does feel nice to be home," Sam said.

"Yes, it does," Jeff replied.

"Muffin must have missed us," Jeff said, pointing down

at their dog. Muffin stared up at them from the bottom of the tree, her tail wagging and thumping on the floor.

The boys climbed carefully down the spiral stairs and shimmied down the rope to the floor. They tiptoed over to the couch so Muffin wouldn't step on them in her excitement.

Jeff reached into the pouch and scooped out some of the dust Mas had given them. He passed a handful to Sam. "When I say three, we both throw it in each other's face. There's nothing in our way here, so when we grow to full size, we won't knock anything over."

"Ready? One, two, and three," Jeff said, and they threw the dust at each other.

Suddenly everything began looking smaller, and then it all stopped.

"We're back to normal size!" Sam exclaimed as Muffin bounded over to them, tail wagging furiously, obviously happy to see them.

Jeff and Sam stood before the tree with their hands tucked in the front of their sweatshirts. Mas and the other ornaments still hung where they had placed them earlier that evening before they left.

As Sam pulled his hand out of his sweatshirt pocket, he felt something small and round sticking to his finger. "Hey, Jeff, look. Isn't this a seed? I thought I'd planted them all, but I must have missed one."

"That's definitely one of the seeds," Jeff said. "We'll have to save it and plant it this spring on the bluff by the beach. That would be a perfect spot. Now let's go to bed."

"I wonder if we'll ever take another adventure like that," Sam said sleepily.

"Probably not," Jeff replied as they started up the stairs to their warm, waiting beds.

If they had only stayed a moment longer, they would have heard Mas whisper, "My two young friends, little do you know, but your adventures are only beginning."

Acknowledgments

I want to thank my wife, Laura, for her understanding during all the hours I spent in front of my computer while I wrote my story.

I want to thank my publisher, Bryna Haynes, for venturing into the fiction side of publishing and taking me on as a new author.

I also want to thank her for finding me the perfect editor, Kimberly Elkins. With her support and help, she not only made me a better writer but also helped make my book a richer and more interesting read.

Lastly, I want to thank my Illustrator, Alyce Wolfe, who captured the spirit of my book through her drawings. She is an incredible artist and illustrator.

About the Author

Jeff grew up in the small town of Epping, New Hampshire. He left when he went into the Army; he completed three years of service for his country and went on to college. At the University of New Hampshire, he met his wife of forty-one years, Laura. They currently live in Magnolia, Massachusetts. He has two sons who have given him four precious grandchildren.

Jeff is a successful business owner of over thirty years and an incredible teller of stories. Afer much prodding from his wife and sons, he finally took up the pen and started writing. Finishing his first book, *Sword and Bow*, he continues to write, and thoroughly enjoys his newfound hobby.

About the Publisher

Founded in 2021 by Bryna Haynes, WorldChangers Media is a boutique publishing company focused on "Ideas for Impact." We know that great books change lives, topple outdated paradigms, and build movements. Our commitment is to deliver superior-quality transformational nonfiction, fiction, and children's books by, and for, the next generation of thought leaders.

Ready to write and publish your book with us? Learn more at www.WorldChangers.Media.

Made in USA - North Chelmsford, MA
1376595_9781955811347
07.17.2023 0823